Cosmo and the Secret Spell

.eth Rees is half Welsh and half English and grew up in land. She went to Glasgow University and qualified as a or in 1990. She is a child and adolescent psychiatrist but ow stopped practising so that she can write full-time. She author of *Cosmo and the Magic Sneeze* and *Cosmo and the Witch Escape*, the bestselling Fairies series (*Fairy Dust*, *Treasure*, *Fairy Dreams*, *Fairy Gold*, *Fairy Rescue* and *Fairy s*) and *Mermaid Magic*, as well as several books for older rs. She lives in London with her partner, Robert, their hter, Eliza, and their two cats, Hattie and Magnus.

Visit www.gwynethrees.com

Gwyneth Rees

Cosmo and the Secret Spell

Illustrated by Samuel Hearn

MACMILLAN CHILDREN'S BOOKS

First published 2008 by Macmillan Children's Books
a division of Macmillan Publishers Limited
20 New Wharf Road, London N1 9RR
Basingstoke and Oxford
Associated companies throughout the world
www.panmacmillan.com

ISBN 978-0-330-44216-9

1 3 5 7 9 8 6 4 2

A CIP catalogue record for this book is available from
the British Library.

Typeset by Intype Libra Ltd
Printed and bound in the UK by CPI Mackays, Chatham ME5 8TD

For my Eliza

1

Cosmo the kitten was now ten months old, which meant that he almost wasn't a kitten any more. He wasn't a fully grown adult cat yet either though, and the witch family he lived with had started to call him a *teenage* cat, which they seemed to think was very funny every time they said it.

'Father, what is a *teenage* cat exactly?' Cosmo asked his father, Mephisto, one morning.

His father looked up from licking his jet-black fur and seemed about to reply, but instead his nose started twitching and the only sound he made was, 'A-A-A-TCHOO!' as he sneezed everywhere.

The noise brought Scarlett (the witch-girl they lived with) running into the room.

'That's your fifth sneeze this morning, Mephisto! And you've been sneezing like that since yesterday. You must have caught a cold and you know what *that* means!'

Mephisto miaowed loudly in protest, because he knew what was coming next. Since witch-cats like Mephisto and Cosmo were known for their powerful magic sneezes (which witches used to help with their

2

spells), a witch-cat with a cold was a very great problem. They might sneeze anywhere at any time, and that meant they might cause all sorts of unintended spells to be activated.

'You'll have to go into quarantine until your cold is over,' Scarlett said firmly. 'I'll make up a nice cosy cat bed for you in the spare room and put the litter tray in there too. We'll bring you plenty of food and drink but you must stay put until you stop sneezing!'

Cosmo looked on while a grumbly Mephisto was carried upstairs by Scarlett. Cosmo's mother wasn't going to like this one bit, he thought, since it meant she was going to have to look after her eight new kittens all by herself.

Cosmo went out through the kitchen cat flap to look for his mother – a beautiful, pure white, short-haired cat called India.

3

It was a lovely sunny day and he soon found her out in the garden trying to wash three of her kittens at the same time. Three more kittens were playing together on the grass nearby while another was chasing a bumblebee despite the fact that India was mewing at it to stop unless it wanted to get stung. The smallest kitten, who looked the most similar to Cosmo, came rushing over to chase his older brother's tail.

'Go away, Kit!' Cosmo hissed, impatiently flicking his tail out of the way.

Whereas Cosmo was almost completely black with four white paws and a white tip to his tail, the youngest kitten had a completely black tail and only three white paws.

The kittens were eight weeks old and full of energy, and Cosmo's parents had yet to give any of them names. Instead the four female kittens were all called Kitty and

the four males were all called Kit – which Cosmo thought was a very unsatisfactory arrangement.

'We're going to have to give them proper names *soon*, aren't we, Mother?' Cosmo said, not for the first time.

'I've told your father that's *his* job,' India miaowed back. 'I'm far too busy to be naming kittens as well as keeping them all clean. Where is he, by the way?'

'Scarlett thinks he's got a cold and she's shutting him up in the spare room,' Cosmo replied.

'What? You mean he's not coming to help me?'

'It's not his fault, Mother,' Cosmo mewed while carefully heading back towards the house as he sensed what was coming next.

'Well, I can't wash eight kittens all at the

same time,' India protested. 'Cosmo, I think you're old enough now to help with keeping them clean so—'

But Cosmo had already disappeared round the side of the house and out into the front garden. It was bad enough trying to keep him*self* clean let alone washing his baby brothers and sisters as well. Besides, he was a teenage cat now, and he was fairly sure that teenage cats did not look after baby kittens. He was no ordinary teenage cat either, he reminded himself. He was a witch-cat, just like his father, and the older he got, the more powerful his own magic sneezes were becoming.

Normally Cosmo would be required to spend at least part of his day with his father, helping Scarlett's parents, Goody and Gabriel, with their spells. But today Goody and Gabriel were leaving to visit their elderly aunt who wanted to see their new baby, Spike (who had been born at around the same time as India's kittens). Scarlett was going to stay with Goody's sister, Bunty, who lived a short broomstick ride away, and the cats were being left on their own with Scarlett popping in regularly to put down fresh food and water and to check up on them.

I wish I could get away from the house for a few days too, Cosmo thought to himself. It's going to be very boring with Scarlett gone and Mother wanting me to help her all the time with the kittens. And just as he thought that, he spotted Albert-of-the-street sauntering along the pavement. Albert-of-the-street was a very handsome adult witch-cat who was all black, apart from his white moustache, which curled up at both ends. As his name suggested, Albert didn't live in a house like Cosmo's family, but roamed free on the streets instead – and right now the idea of having that much freedom greatly appealed to Cosmo.

'Albert, wait for me!' Cosmo called out, bounding across his front garden to catch up with the older cat.

He quickly explained his situation, and Albert immediately invited him to hang out with him. 'I can't think of anything worse than being cooped up in a house filled with other cats,' he said. 'I can teach you to be a street cat, no problem. Just follow me.'

As they walked along together, Albert explained to Cosmo that being a street cat on no account meant that one had to *sleep* on the street. 'I have many places to sleep,' Albert explained, 'though usually not one of them is my home for more than a few nights at a time. The exception is that for the last few weeks I have been sleeping in the same place every night. Ever since a certain bad witch we both know got sent to prison, I have been sleeping in her vacant house – Sticky-End Cottage.'

'Selina Slaughter's house?' Cosmo said in alarm. 'But doesn't that make you feel . . . ?' He shuddered, thinking about Selina Slaughter and how she had very nearly succeeded in pulling off an extremely evil spell only a few weeks before.

'Scared?' Albert said, looking sideways at Cosmo. 'Not at all, my friend. The house is empty apart from Selina's white mice, who keep well out of my way as you can imagine!' He chuckled. 'They used to act as spies for her in exchange for having a nice warm place to sleep and plenty of cheese to eat. Now they just sit around the house all day long with nothing to do except pay her a visit in prison from time to time. Not that they were as grateful as I expected when I offered to move in for a while and keep them company. I did tell them that I rarely eat mice, but they still got into a total flap. Silly creatures.'

'Maybe some good witches will come and live in Sticky-End Cottage soon,' Cosmo said hopefully.

'Perhaps – though that cottage always

11

seems to attract bad witches – the Broom sisters lived there before Selina, and remember how bad *they* were? One of them's in prison with Selina now, I believe. Still, luckily the Broom sisters had a cat and so there's a cat flap in the back door, which makes it very easy for me to get in and out.'

'I'm not sure I want to sleep in Sticky-End Cottage tonight, Albert,' Cosmo mewed. 'Isn't there somewhere else we could stay instead?'

'Street cats can't be choosy, Cosmo,' Albert said sternly. 'So if you're going to be fussy you'd better go back to your parents right now.'

Cosmo did his best to feel brave. 'No, it's all right. I really do want to learn how to be a street cat like you, Albert.'

'Then follow me.' And Albert led him down into an open sewage pipe, which he had discovered was a handy shortcut underneath the main road. And Cosmo felt very brave indeed as he thought about what his mother would say if she could see him – and smell him – right now.

It took them quite some time to reach Sticky-End Cottage, since Albert made several stops on the way to steal titbits of food from various houses with open windows. But finally they arrived at Selina's old house, where, to Albert's obvious surprise, a large removal van was parked outside.

Two white mice were scurrying away from the house as they approached it and Albert called out after them, 'Who's moving in?'

'Selina's son and his pregnant wife,' one of the mice squeaked back at him. (Most cats understood a bit of mouse language and vice versa.)

'Surely there's no need to run away?' Albert said in surprise. 'Selina let you live with her, didn't she? Surely her son will do the same?'

'Yes, but his wife has food cravings and one of them is for mice on toast!' the mouse explained. And with that they both vanished into the bushes.

'Well,' said Albert, looking at one of the

removal men as he carried a large dog kennel round to the back of the house, 'it looks like this might not be the best place to stay tonight after all.'

'But where else can we go?' Cosmo asked.

'Another of my favourite stopover places is not far from here,' Albert said. 'Come on. We'll go and stay with my friend the Frog-Witch instead. You've probably heard of her.'

'No, I haven't,' said Cosmo. 'Is she famous then?'

'She's the leading expert on frog magic in this country, but she's also a bit of a recluse and rather eccentric. She never minds me curling up for the night on her sofa, and I'm sure she'll let you stay too. All you have to remember is that on no account must you touch any of her frogs.'

15

Cosmo felt a little worried at the thought of being in a room with lots of frogs that he wasn't allowed to touch. After all, it was almost impossible to resist the urge to give a jumpy frog just a *little* tap with your paw. But Albert seemed unconcerned about that as he led Cosmo away from Sticky-End Cottage and back along the street.

2

The Frog-Witch's home turned out to be only two streets away in a road full of very large houses, several of which had the pink chimneys (invisible to humans) that showed they belonged to witches. As Albert led the way up the driveway, Cosmo saw several ponds in the front garden.

'She keeps a lot of her frogs outside so that they can enjoy a more natural habitat,' Albert told him. 'You should see her back garden! It's so full of ponds that there's hardly any space left to walk.'

As they approached the house they heard raised voices coming from inside.

'She must have a visitor,' Albert said. 'Come on. There's a kitchen window she always leaves open round the back. We'll

17

get in that way.' But before they could veer off to the side of the house the front door was flung open and a very angry-looking dark-haired young man stepped outside.

'You'll regret this!' he shouted back at the stout elderly witch who had followed him to the front door. 'You're an old fool and it won't be long before you see just how stupid you've been! But then it will be too late!' He strode down the path, narrowly missing stamping on Cosmo's tail as the cats scurried to get out of his way.

As the front gate crashed shut behind

the Frog-Witch's visitor, Albert came out of his hiding place and ran to greet the witch, who was looking quite shaken, at the door.

'Oh, Albert, it's you,' she murmured as he rubbed against her legs. 'Do you know, I think I need to sit down.'

'I've brought a friend,' Albert mewed to her, at which point Cosmo came bounding up the path to join them. 'Cosmo, this is the Frog-Witch.'

Cosmo mewed his politest greeting at the harassed-looking witch, who Cosmo saw had a large frog perched on one shoulder, another two poking out of one of the pockets in her cloak, and a third that looked like it had made a nest in her bushy grey hair. Albert was right, he thought. She did seem rather eccentric.

'You'd better come inside and we'll lock the door behind us. I don't think he'll come

19

back, but you never know.' The Frog-Witch shuddered as she glanced towards the gate.

'Who is he?' Albert asked her once they were safely inside the house.

It was then that Cosmo realized the Frog-Witch was one of the few clever witches who understood cat language, because she answered, 'A young male witch who thinks he knows better than I do! He knew all about my secret spell, Albert! And I don't know how he found out!'

'*What* secret spell?' Cosmo asked curiously.

The Frog-Witch narrowed her eyes. 'The less anyone else knows about that the better. I know how gossipy you cats are! In fact, I wouldn't be surprised if it wasn't a cat who's been telling tales to that dreadful young man.'

'Well, it wasn't me,' Albert assured her.

'I haven't breathed a word about it to anyone!' He turned to Cosmo and added, 'It's extremely secret, you see.'

'It's an extremely secret spell that I'm very near to perfecting,' the Frog-Witch murmured. 'And when I do, it will change the boundaries of witchcraft forever!'

As she spoke she led them through to the back of the house, where the noise of croaking could be heard. In fact, Cosmo had never heard so much croaking. There were deep frog croaks mixed with high chirps, long grunts and short ribbits, and as they entered an enormous living room, Cosmo saw that there were frogs everywhere. There were frogs perched on the backs of the sofa and armchairs, and sitting on the coffee table (where a large dish of water had been left for them to bathe in). There were even more frogs hopping about the carpet and one was

resting in a large greenery-filled cage with a small artificial pond inside.

'I try to let them come and go as they please,' the Frog-Witch explained, seeing Cosmo looking at the cage, 'but I do have one frog that I have to keep under lock and key because he is extremely precious.'

Cosmo stared up at the large cage, which contained a very handsome green frog who had a sprig of ivy on its head and who was croaking loudly at them in a cross sort of manner.

'That one used to be a prince,' Albert told Cosmo. 'That's why he's so cross – and why he likes to wear that ivy crown all the time.'

'Wow!' Cosmo exclaimed, because although he knew all about princes being turned into frogs by wicked spells, he had never before met one who it had actually

23

happened to. 'But can't the Frog-Witch just find a princess to kiss him and turn him back into a prince again?' he asked.

'Don't be silly, Cosmo!' Albert said. 'A kiss from a princess can't *really* turn a frog back into a prince. That only happens in fairy tales!'

'Oh,' Cosmo mewed in surprise. 'So can't *anybody* help him then?'

'The Frog-Witch is his only hope,' Albert said.

Cosmo glanced at the Frog-Witch, who was now cooing dotingly as she tried to tickle under the chin of a frog that was poking its head out of one of her long sleeves.

Albert lowered his voice and added, 'She may *seem* a bit loopy, but she really is one of the cleverest witches you're ever likely to meet, Cosmo.'

'Is she?' Cosmo murmured.

'Oh yes. You know how, in the local Witch Prison, all the bad witches are fitted with a special magic tag that means they get turned into frogs if they try and escape?'

Cosmo nodded.

'Well, it was the Frog-Witch who invented those tags.'

'That *is* clever,' Cosmo agreed excitedly, and he went on to tell Albert about the witch he used to live with – Sybil – who had got turned into a frog when *she* had tried to escape from prison. Sybil – who had been very bad indeed – had owned the house Cosmo's family had lived in before the Two-Shoes family moved in – and whereas Scarlett, Goody and Gabriel were good witches, Sybil had only been pretending to be good. Cosmo was the one who had exposed how bad she really was – and she had vowed to get him back for getting her sent to Witch Prison. But when she had tried to use even more bad magic to escape from prison, the spell had gone wrong, and instead of escaping she had been turned into a large, angry frog. And since it was a well-known fact that no witch who had been turned into a frog had ever been turned back again, everyone assumed that Sybil was now gone for good.

'I expect she's a very *ugly* frog,' Cosmo said to himself, and he shivered at the thought of ever meeting Sybil again – even if it was only in frog-form.

The Frog-Witch was sitting down on the sofa now, with a large croaking frog on each knee. 'Frogs are *such* soothing creatures to have around,' she said, sighing contentedly as a third plump frog jumped up on to her lap. 'I know most witches prefer cats, but I must say I find the sound of frogs croaking every bit as restful as the purr of a cat.'

Albert gave Cosmo a wink as he jumped up on to the nearest unoccupied chair and curled up in readiness for his afternoon nap. 'Like I told you – she's frog mad,' he murmured. 'But she doesn't mind the odd cat visiting now and again. Find yourself a chair and get comfortable, why don't you?'

However, Cosmo was beginning to find all the chirping and croaking and frog-song around him extremely *un*soothing – not to mention the continuous hopping and jumping that was going on everywhere in the room.

'I've been thinking . . .' he told Albert. 'Mother might get quite worried about me if I don't go home soon. I know I said I wanted to be a street cat like you, but I think I'd better go and *tell* Mother that I'm planning on leaving home first.'

27

'Very wise,' Albert agreed, closing his eyes and curling one paw in front of them to block out any light that might spoil his afternoon slumber. 'You go and speak to her about it, and if you still want to be a street cat tomorrow then come back and meet me here.'

It was just as well that Cosmo had such a good sense of direction, because Albert clearly wasn't inclined to leave his chair in order to show the younger cat the way back. But Cosmo never went anywhere without making sure he knew the way back home again, and luckily he had made sure he rubbed his scent up against several lamp posts and gateposts on the way as a marker.

He got back to find his mother in the front garden, yowling at the top of her voice, and at first he thought she had discovered he was missing and was calling for *him*. But he soon realized that she was worried for another reason.

'I've lost Kit!' she told him as soon as he joined her. '*You* might be old enough to go off on your own all day – but *he* isn't! Goody and Gabriel have already left with Spike, and Scarlett has gone to Bunty's house, so I've no one to help me look for him.'

'I'll help you,' Cosmo said immediately. 'Which Kit is it?'

'The smallest one. He's always trying to follow you, Cosmo, and I think he might have gone off looking for you today! You haven't seen him, have you?'

'Of course not or I'd have brought him straight home again,' Cosmo mewed. 'Don't worry, Mother. I know all the places kittens like to explore around here. I'll find him for you!'

29

'Your father's still in quarantine and I have to go and look after the other kittens,' India replied, 'so it would be a big help if you *could* look for him, Cosmo.'

Without saying anything else, Cosmo hurried round to the back of the house to begin his search. The back garden was the place to start, he was sure, because he had seen the smallest kitten heading off towards the bottom of their back garden the day before, only to be called back sternly by their father. And he would have heard Kit or smelt him if Kit had followed him along the road with Albert today, because young kittens were not very good at being stealthy and invisible like older cats.

When Cosmo reached the bottom flower-bed he soon spotted something that made him certain his younger brother had been here – paw prints. They were tiny, baby-kitten-sized paw prints and they led across the dirt, round the same rose bush twice, and on through the flower-bed as far as the fence that separated their garden from the next one. There was a very small hole in the fence where the paw prints ended. Kit must have gone through that hole and into the next garden, Cosmo thought.

Cosmo was too big to squeeze through the gap himself, so he jumped right over the fence instead, and found himself in the flower-bed of the house that backed on to theirs, which belonged to a rather excitable Yorkie dog called Ramses. In the middle of the Yorkie's lawn, Cosmo could see the garden pond, which he himself had found very exciting as a young kitten – and sure enough, there was Kit at the very edge of it, tapping at the water. Cosmo was about to call out to him when something unexpected happened.

31

From the
undergrowth
around the
pond, just behind
where Kit was
standing, an
enormous
frog suddenly
leaped out
and pounced on
to Kit's back – and the
tiny kitten got such a fright that he toppled
forward, right into the pond.

Cosmo raced towards the pond as Kit
splashed helplessly in the water. Kit couldn't
swim and he would drown unless Cosmo
saved him. But Cosmo couldn't swim either
– so what was he going to do?

He reached the pond to find Kit barely
afloat in the middle of the water, too far

out from the edge for Cosmo to reach him by extending a paw. If he wanted to save his little brother, Cosmo would have to jump into the water too. But how could he stay afloat himself if he couldn't swim? Cosmo suddenly remembered seeing Ramses swimming across this pond one hot afternoon during the summer. (Ramses had moved his front and back paws like paddles and kept his chin up above the water as he had moved forward, Cosmo remembered.) Ramses was a similar shape to Cosmo and *he* hadn't sunk – so maybe if Cosmo did exactly what he had done, then he would be able to swim across the pond too. Cosmo had never seen a cat swim before – in fact most cats hated water and avoided getting wet whenever they could – but he didn't see why a cat shouldn't be able to stay afloat if a dog could.

33

'Try and keep still, Kit. I'm coming to rescue you!' Cosmo yowled, and before he could change his mind he plunged into the pond and started to move all four paws as fast as he could, in just the same way he had seen Ramses do. Miraculously, it worked!

Kit was right in front of him. The kitten was almost completely submerged, so Cosmo had no choice but to grab the first bit of Kit's fur he could get his teeth into – and keep hold of it, while paddling as hard as he could towards the other side of the pond.

Cosmo was exhausted by the time he reached dry land, but he still found the strength to haul the younger kitten out of the water. Kit was totally bedraggled, trembling with shock and spluttering water as he lay on his side beside Cosmo.

Suddenly, out of the corner of his eye, Cosmo saw a large ugly frog glaring at him fiercely from the undergrowth.

He turned his head sharply, but there was nothing there.

Cosmo told himself he must be imagining things. After all, the frog that had given Kit such a fright and made him fall into the

35

pond was probably long gone by now and completely unaware of the chaos it had caused.

Kit was opening his eyes and starting to whimper. 'Don't worry, Kit, you're safe now,' Cosmo told him, before licking the pondweed from his little brother's face.

And from far back under the bushes, the large ugly frog – which had a very unfroglike wart on its face – watched them in angry silence.

3

Cosmo watched as India licked her smallest kitten until she was satisfied that all the nasty pond water was completely gone. 'You were very brave to jump in and rescue him, Cosmo,' she said between licks. 'I'm very proud of you.'

'Yes, but he's even more wet now, Mother,' Cosmo pointed out, because he couldn't help feeling that his mother went a bit too far where licking was concerned. After all, the pond hadn't been *that* dirty.

India eyed Cosmo's fur, which was also still damp from his plunge into the water, and Cosmo realized she was thinking of licking *him* clean too. 'I'm going to tell Father what happened,' he said, but before he could bound away up the stairs, the cat flap opened and Cosmo's friend Mia appeared.

Mia was a young tabby cat, the same age as Cosmo, who lived next door with her mother, Professor Felina, and a very doting human called Amy. She was clearly bursting to tell him something so he decided to let her speak first before telling her about his experience at the pond.

'Cosmo, you'll never guess what's happened!' she miaowed excitedly. And before he could even *try* and guess, she continued, 'Amy's got a boyfriend! Mother's very worried about it because Amy is completely in love with him and Mother says that a human who's in love is often a lot less doting on her cats than she ought to be. This morning Amy forgot to fill up our food bowl before the Crunchy-munchies ran out! Can you imagine?'

'Wow!' Cosmo mewed in reply. 'What's he like?'

'You'll see for yourself in a minute. Before Goody left she came round to our house to ask Amy if she'd look in on all of you this evening. Scarlett and her aunt are coming in to see you tomorrow, but she wanted you checked up on before then as Mephisto has a cold. Anyway, when Amy told Maurice – that's his name – he insisted on doing it for her. Mother thought I'd better come and tell you so that you didn't wonder who he was. He should be here any minute.'

'But it's not evening yet,' Cosmo said, looking out of the window at the late-afternoon sky.

'I know. Mother thinks that he's just trying to impress Amy by being super keen to help out.' (The professor-cat was an expert in the study of Human Behaviour

39

– or Humanology as she liked to call it – so she was very good at analysing the ways of humans.)

'I'd better go and tell Father,' Cosmo said. 'He won't like it if a stranger suddenly walks in on him – especially if he's in the middle of using his litter tray or something!'

'Mother tried to tell Amy that,' Mia replied, 'but Amy doesn't understand cat language, no matter how hard Mother tries to teach her.' (The professor-cat was also an expert in foreign languages, including Human, and she often tried to spell out human words for Amy using scratch marks on the back of the sofa or Crunchy-munchies spilt on the kitchen floor – but Amy never seemed to appreciate Felina's efforts.)

Cosmo was about to go upstairs when the cats heard the front door opening and

Mia mewed, 'That must be Maurice now.'

Footsteps could soon be heard moving around in the hall, then in the living room and then in the dining room. 'Why is he looking all round the house instead of coming straight through to the kitchen?' Mia said.

Then they heard Maurice open the cupboard under the stairs and rummage around in there, grumbling impatiently, 'Where *are* you?'

There was something familiar about his voice, but before Cosmo had time to work out what it was, Amy's boyfriend entered the kitchen.

Cosmo let out a startled miaow, because the figure who stood in front of them was the same young man Cosmo had seen coming out of the Frog-Witch's house earlier that afternoon!

41

Cosmo felt the fur on his tail start to bush up as their visitor gave the cats a dismissive glance before heading straight past them to the back door. He unlocked it with the key that Goody had left there, muttering, 'You're much more likely to be out here somewhere, I suppose . . .'

As soon as he had gone, Mia exclaimed, 'That's a *very* strange way for a human to behave!'

'He's not a human – he's a witch!' Cosmo miaowed, before telling them all about his visit to the Frog-Witch.

'What – or who – can he be looking for here?' India asked, sounding worried. 'Oh dear – I wish your father wasn't shut up in the spare room.'

'I'd better follow him and see what he's up to,' Cosmo said.

'I'll come too!' Mia mewed.

'Be careful, both of you,' India told them, and she turned to her new kittens and told them very sternly that they must all get inside the cat basket and stay there. Then she hurried upstairs to tell Mephisto through the door what was going on.

Out in the garden, Cosmo and Mia crept across the grass, keeping their bodies low as they stalked the young witch, who had reached the bottom of the garden and seemed very interested in what was underneath the bushes there.

He muttered to himself, before suddenly looking at his watch and frowning when he saw the time. Then he turned and walked swiftly back across the lawn as the two cats hid behind a bush so that he wouldn't spot them.

'We've got to keep following him,' Cosmo said. 'Come on!'

They followed Maurice round to the front of the house and along the pavement as far as a bus stop in the next street. Presently a bus pulled up at the stop and Maurice climbed aboard.

'I wonder where he's going,' Mia said.

'That's the bus you catch if you want to visit the Witch Prison,' Cosmo told her. 'It drops you off right outside. I wonder if he's going to visit somebody there.'

'What shall we do now?' Mia asked as they watched the bus disappear round the corner.

'I think you should tell your mother that Maurice is a witch, not a human, and see if she can find out more about him by nosing through his stuff. Has he *got* any stuff at your house?'

'Oh yes – lots of magazines and things! They're in Amy's spare room and he's asked her not to touch any of them.'

'Well, see what you can find. I'm going to visit the Frog-Witch again to see if *she* can tell me any more about him.'

'Be careful, Cosmo,' Mia mewed.

'You too – I'll meet you back at my house later, OK?'

And they rubbed noses to say goodbye.

What neither Cosmo nor Mia realized was

45

that they had been followed to the bus stop. Cosmo's eight brothers and sisters had sneaked out of the cat basket after their mother had gone upstairs, and now they were having a great time stalking their older brother.

By the time Cosmo reached the Frog-Witch's house, he *still* hadn't noticed that they were behind him, which was partly because he was more lost in his own thoughts

than usual, and partly because the smallest kitten was actually very good at directing the others to move forward or stay put at the appropriate times as they tailed Cosmo.

As Cosmo found the open kitchen window at the back of the Frog-Witch's house, the smallest kitten had already spotted another opening at the side of the house that was at just the right level for the kittens to reach.

'Look!' he mewed as he stuck his head inside it. 'There's some sort of slide attached to the other side of *this* window!' In fact it was more of an air vent than a window – and it had rather a strange smell coming out of it – but it was easily big enough for the kittens to climb through. 'Hey!' he protested, as the other seven bigger kittens pushed him out of the way to inspect the opening themselves.

Inside the house, Cosmo was miaowing

47

to try and attract the attention of Albert or the Frog-Witch. They didn't seem to be there, and after checking the ground floor and finding it occupied only by frogs, he spotted a door in the hall that looked like it led down to the basement. Gingerly he hooked it open with his paw and headed down a flight of stone steps until he came to another door, which he nudged with his nose until it creaked open and he found himself inside some sort of laboratory. On various bench tops all around the room were glass jugs and jars filled with different coloured liquids, some of which were giving off rainbow-coloured steam as they bubbled away.

The Frog-Witch was standing at a bench on the far side of the room, fiddling with some sort of strange contraption that consisted of a series of tubes leading back to a large

cauldron, from which gold and green steam was billowing out. The last tube led into an enclosed plastic incubator, inside which a white mouse was sitting nibbling at a piece of cheese. There was also a tube leading out through the container roof, upwards and out through the top of the basement wall, which, the witch now explained to the mouse, would be its source of fresh air throughout the whole experiment.

'Good, because it's very smelly in here,' the mouse squeaked.

'It *is* rather a stinky sort of spell, I'm afraid,' the Frog-Witch agreed apologetically. 'I'm *very* grateful to you for volunteering. And rest assured, there's no need to worry if you don't enjoy being a frog, because I will be turning you back into a mouse again very soon.'

Cosmo's ears pricked up at that. Everyone

knew that any animal who had been turned into a frog, could never be turned back again, so what was going on?

The Frog-Witch stepped back from the apparatus, clearly still unaware of Cosmo's presence as she reached up to touch a red button on the wall. As she pressed the button there was a noise inside the cauldron – and even more noise from inside the series of tubes – before gold-coloured sparkling smoke started to billow out into the incubator.

Cosmo watched the sparkly smoke completely engulf the mouse and then, very suddenly and silently, in the time that it took him to blink once, the white mouse had been changed into a small green frog.

The whole incubator had now filled up with gold smoke and the frog was starting to make a strange noise, midway

51

between a choke and a croak. Then there was a loud thudding noise from the air tube that ran down into the incubator from the top of the wall, and suddenly – to the Frog-Witch's obvious amazement – one *kitten* after another came hurtling down it! And as they breathed in the golden smoke inside the incubator, they instantly got turned into frogs too!

'Oh my goodness!' the Frog-Witch exclaimed,

rushing to press the red button that turned the apparatus off.

Cosmo yowled with fright as he saw what was happening, and that's when the Frog-Witch noticed him for the first time. 'What are *you* doing here?' she burst out. Then she turned back to her apparatus and held in her breath before opening the door of the incubator, just as the last of Cosmo's siblings was hurtling down the tube. She managed to catch it in time to whisk it out before it breathed in any of the smoke, then she slammed the door shut and carried it out of the basement, shooing Cosmo ahead of her.

'Those are my brothers and sisters!' Cosmo miaowed when they reached the top of the basement stairs. 'We can't just leave them there.'

The Frog-Witch looked angry as she

53

replied, 'Your brothers and sisters nearly ruined my experiment!' She placed the kitten she had saved on the floor and looked down at it sternly. 'I suppose you found the air-vent opening and thought you'd use it as a slide, did you?'

'We were following Cosmo,' the kitten whimpered, and Cosmo saw that it was the smallest kitten – the one he had already had to rescue once that day.

'Mother told you to stay in your basket, Kit,' he mewed at it crossly. 'What's she going to say when she hears that all the others have been turned into frogs?' And as he thought about having to tell his mother what had happened he began to feel like whimpering himself.

'You know, it's really not so bad being a frog,' the Frog-Witch said, trying to cheer him up. 'In a minute I shall go down and give them some nice slugs to eat. They'll like that!'

'But they're *not* frogs!' Cosmo burst out. 'They're *kittens*!'

The Frog-Witch looked unperturbed. 'And they will be again. Don't worry. Remember the secret spell I told you about – the one I have been working on for years? Well, it's ready at last.' She looked very proud as she announced, 'I am the first witch ever to invent a spell that can turn frogs back into whatever creature they started out as!'

'But that's impossible!' Cosmo exclaimed.

'Plenty of witches before me have tried it, and none have succeeded, that is true!' the Frog-Witch agreed. 'But I am not called the Frog-Witch for nothing! No one knows more about frog magic than I do! And that is why I will succeed where every other witch has failed! Just think, my frog prince will soon become a true prince once again! And all those kittens will be transformed back to their original selves as well!'

'So . . . so do you know for *sure* that you can do it?' Cosmo asked nervously.

'I am absolutely positive! And after tomorrow, when I change my volunteer mouse – and all those kittens – back to their normal selves again, everyone else will know it too!'

'Do you *have* to wait until tomorrow?' Cosmo asked, thinking it would be much better if she could change the kittens back now, without his mother ever having to know what had happened to them.

'I'm afraid so,' the Frog-Witch replied. 'The new frog-form must be left intact for at *least* twenty-four hours before it is interfered with by any further magic.'

56

At that moment Albert-of-the-street appeared from upstairs, where he had gone to find himself a more comfortable bed and had been rewarded by a peaceful slumber on the Frog-Witch's best duvet (which she always tried to keep frog-free for fear of squashing incidents). He yawned as he greeted them. 'Such a restful house,' he purred.

And the Frog-Witch let out an impatient sigh before shooing all three cats out of her house, telling them not to come back until she sent for them.

4

While Cosmo had been at the Frog-Witch's house, the witches in the local Witch Prison had been enjoying their weekly visiting time.

One witch in particular – Murdina Broom – was on floor-mopping duty, since she never had any visitors. Her friends (who had all been bad witches like herself) had deserted her long ago, and her only relative was her sister, Belinda, who had unfortunately been turned into a frog after trying to escape from prison the year before. Now Murdina was keen to make friends with Selina Slaughter, because she was a rather clever and influential witch who had been sent to prison because she had tried to help Sybil escape. Selina had been a great pal of Sybil's and she had been very cross when her best friend had been turned into a frog while escaping – which hadn't been part of her plan at all.

Selina currently had a visitor that Murdina didn't recognize – a young male witch with dark hair – who was sitting across the table from Selina, listening very carefully to whatever it was that she was telling him.

Murdina decided to edge closer with her bucket and mop to try and hear what was being said. As she reached the table next to Selina's she pretended to notice a spillage and started to mop more energetically.

'That's all very well, but how do I find her?' the young man was saying.

'I've told you! She'll return to somewhere close to where she used to live. It will probably be somewhere wet and slimy like a garden pond!' Selina lowered her voice even more, so that Murdina had to get even closer to

59

hear her. 'Now as to the rest of our plan – is everything ready?'

'Yes – I shall go to the Frog-Witch's house as soon as I leave here.'

'Excellent!' Selina started to say something else, but broke off as she noticed Murdina listening to them. 'What do you think you're doing?' she hissed. 'This is a private conversation!'

'I'm just making sure the floor is clean for your young visitor,' Murdina said, smiling and showing off her two rows of perfectly crooked yellow teeth. 'Aren't you going to introduce us?'

'No I'm not!' Selina snarled. 'Now get lost!' And she stood up and gave Murdina a nasty shove.

Murdina shrieked as she fell backwards and landed in the bucket of dirty water she had been using to clean the floor. The other witches

cackled with laughter as she struggled to get her rear end out of the bucket – with Selina cackling the loudest of all. And it was then that Murdina changed her mind about wanting to be Selina's friend.

By the time Murdina had extracted herself, visiting time was over and the young man was getting ready to leave. Murdina was none the wiser as to who he was or exactly what he and Selina had been plotting together. She was certain they had

61

been plotting *something* though – and she intended to make it her business to find out what.

When Cosmo arrived home with Kit and Albert, he was very relieved to find that his mother wasn't there. Of course he knew he would eventually have to tell her what had happened to the kittens, but he was more than happy to put it off for a little while longer.

'What's that?' Kit asked in alarm as they entered the house, because a strange grunting noise was coming from upstairs.

'That's Father snoring,' Cosmo told him. 'We probably shouldn't wake him up yet, since he's got such a bad cold.' (He was dreading breaking the news to his father, who had a very quick temper and who Cosmo feared might blame *him* for everything.)

'We *have* to wake him up,' Albert said firmly. 'If it were my kittens who had been changed into frogs, I'd want to know immediately.' And he led the way upstairs.

The door to the spare room was shut and it was impossible for an ordinary cat to push it open. But that wasn't a problem, since neither Albert or Cosmo were ordinary cats. 'One of us will have to do a magic sneeze on the doorknob,' Albert announced. 'Stand back, Kit, and let Cosmo show you how it's done.'

Kit watched with excitement as Cosmo sniffed about on the landing for some dust to breathe in. Dust was very good at tickling the inside of your nose and making you sneeze, and since the Two-Shoes family were not fond of housework, he soon found enough dust to do the job.

'A-A-A-TCHOO!' sneezed Cosmo, lifting up his chin so that his sneeze particles

63

were directed upwards at the door, causing the knob to turn magically by itself and the door to swing open. 'If it's that easy for a witch-cat to open the door, why didn't Father just open it with a magic sneeze himself?' Kit mewed as he followed the two bigger cats into the room.

Nobody answered him because Mephisto had just woken up, and now he was jumping down from the bed to greet Albert with a soft warning growl. He knew the other witch-cat well, and was therefore a lot *less* growly than he might have been, but it was still most irritating that another male cat should enter his territory unannounced.

'Sorry to burst in on you, mate, but this is an emergency,' Albert said quickly. 'I'm afraid there's been a bit of a mishap with a spell. Cosmo will explain.'

Mephisto turned to Cosmo. 'Well?'

'It's . . . it's the k-kittens, Father,' Cosmo began nervously. 'They . . . followed me and I . . . I didn't know they were there, and they . . . they accidentally got turned into frogs.'

Mephisto's whiskers jerked forward in alarm and he let out an involuntary hiss.

'You see, we all followed Cosmo to the Frog-Witch's house,' Kit piped up (a little too enthusiastically), 'and we found this big tube thing that led inside. And we thought it was a slide, so we slid down it and landed

65

inside this funny room that was full of gold smoke! The smoke turned all the others into frogs, and it would have turned me into one too, but the Frog-Witch rescued me just in time! But it's OK about the others because—'

Mephisto let out such a loud second hiss that Kit instantly clammed up, jumping backwards in fright.

'From what Cosmo told me, it was a tragic accident,' Albert chipped in solemnly, 'not intentional on the part of the Frog-Witch at all.'

'That's right, Father – and the Frog-Witch says she's got a new spell that will turn all the frogs back into kittens again,' Cosmo added quickly.

Mephisto remained speechless as the reality of the situation sank in. Seven of his eight new kittens were gone – victims of the strongest of all magic spells! And every witch-cat knew that there was no way of reversing such a spell, despite what Cosmo might have been told.

'The Frog-Witch has been working on a secret reversing spell for years,' Albert said, guessing what the other cat was thinking. 'You never know, Mephisto – she might be able to do it.'

Mephisto seemed about to reply when his ears pricked up at the sound of a noise downstairs. 'That's India. She's been out looking for the kittens in the garden. She wanted me to go with her, but I told her Scarlett had put a spell on the door knob so that it couldn't be sneezed open.' He frowned. 'When she sees how easily *you* got in I'll never hear the last of it!'

'I don't understand, Father,' Kit said, wide-eyed. 'Why did you pretend to Mother that you couldn't open the door if you *could* open it really?'

'Because I wanted some peace and quiet away from you kittens,' Mephisto retorted. 'Though clearly this family can't do without me for the shortest time without a complete catastrophe occurring!' He began to pace up and down the room angrily, swishing his long black tail from side to side – which always helped him to think. 'Cosmo, I don't want your mother to hear about this until I've spoken to the Frog-Witch myself. You must tell her that the kittens are staying with a witch friend of mine who is taking very good care of them. Meanwhile I will go with Albert to see if anything can be done.'

'But I'm no good at lying,' Cosmo protested. 'Mother will never believe me!'

'I have a very good lying spell you can borrow if you like,' Albert suggested helpfully. 'I always keep a little of it on my paw so that I can use it when I'm begging for food. It gives me a *much* more desperate-sounding miaow when I'm pretending to a human that I haven't had anything to eat for days.' And he offered Cosmo his right paw to lick.

Cosmo took rather a big lick and Albert withdrew his paw crossly, grumbling that he hadn't meant the younger cat to lick off *that* much of the magic ointment. Cosmo, whose tongue was feeling remarkably tingly all of a sudden, mewed indignantly in reply, 'But I hardly licked off *any* of it!' (Which obviously meant that the magic was working already.)

'Albert, you'd better race ahead of me down the stairs so that I can pretend I'm chasing you out of the house!' Mephisto instructed. 'That will stop India from asking me any questions.'

As they heard India approaching, Mephisto growled, 'NOW, ALBERT!' and

69

the two cats shot off at lightning speed, nearly flattening India against the wall as they raced past her on the stairs.

'Cosmo! Kit!' India exclaimed as soon as she saw them on the landing. 'What's going on? I thought your father couldn't sneeze open that door? And who was that other cat?'

'That was Albert-of-the-street, Mother,' Cosmo told her. 'We opened the door for Father by . . . by sneezing on it together – two magic sneezes are stronger than one, you see. But then they had a bit of an argument.' He was surprised by how convincing his lying sounded as he added, 'And the other kittens aren't here but they're quite safe. They're staying with a witch friend of Father's.'

India looked puzzled. 'But *why*?'

'She wants to have one of them as her witch-cat when they get older, so she wants to see which one she likes best.'

'But we don't know yet if *any* of them will become witch-cats,' India answered. 'You know very well that we can't find out until they undergo the special witch-cat test when they are six months old.'

'I know, Mother,' Cosmo continued glibly as the lying spell made the words tumble from his mouth, 'but you see, this witch is looking to fill her house with *all* kinds of cats. She says she likes us as much for our beauty and charming personalities as for our ability to help with magic spells.'

'Which witch *is* this, Cosmo?' India asked, sounding amazed. 'She sounds too good to be true!'

Cosmo took a deep breath, ready to continue with his elaborate lie, but unfortunately Kit chose that moment to try *his* hand at lying too. 'She's called the

11

Frog-Witch, Mother,' Kit mewed, 'and don't worry, because she *hasn't* turned all the other kittens into frogs!'

India stared at him, looking horrified. 'Into *frogs*?'

'I said she *hasn't* turned them into frogs,' Kit repeated, a little alarmed at the way his mother was starting to growl under her breath. 'I mean, it's not as if they all got caught up in an experiment that went wrong, or anything like that.'

'Shut up, Kit,' Cosmo hissed, but it was too late.

India pounced on her youngest kitten and held him down firmly with her paw as she miaowed at the top of her voice that she wanted to know *right now* what had really happened to his brothers and sisters.

5

After Kit had blurted out everything to their mother, India was inconsolable until Cosmo reassured her that the Frog-Witch had promised to turn the kittens back to normal again by the following day. (Fortunately, since India wasn't a witch-cat herself, she didn't know enough about magic to realize that such a spell was virtually impossible – and that it would take a miracle, or a very major breakthrough in frog magic, for it to actually come about.)

'I can't believe that your father tried to keep this from me,' she hissed as she followed Cosmo and Kit along the pavement, having insisted that they take her to the Frog-Witch's house immediately.

'I think he just didn't want you to get

upset until he'd had a chance to find out for himself if the Frog-Witch really has invented a reversal spell,' Cosmo said.

'What do you mean – *invented*?' India demanded. 'I thought you just said there was one in existence already!'

'Er . . .' Cosmo found that he didn't know what to say – which probably meant that his lying spell had worn off.

Fortunately they had nearly arrived at their destination, so instead of answering

her, he pointed out the street where the Frog-Witch lived. The door of her house was wide open, and when they stepped inside they were greeted by the deafening

75

croaking of frogs, who all seemed very alarmed. There was no sign of Albert or Mephisto – or of the Frog-Witch herself – as they padded through the house, with India keeping a firm eye on Kit the whole time to check he didn't wander off and fall into the kitchen cauldron or somewhere equally dangerous.

The door to the basement was open and Cosmo guessed that the Frog-Witch was probably in her laboratory. 'Come on, Mother,' he mewed, 'the kittens are down here too – only remember that they won't *look* like kittens.'

The sight that greeted him when they stepped inside the basement room made him growl in fright. The Frog-Witch wasn't there, and the whole room looked like it had been turned upside down. The cauldron had been pushed over on to its side, and the elaborate system of pipes and tubes had

broken apart and lay in pieces on the floor. There was broken glass everywhere, and spilt liquids of all different colours that India immediately yowled at Kit not to touch. The Frog-Witch's high wooden stool was broken, as if somebody had smashed it against the wall, and the plastic incubator where the frogs had last been was overturned with its door open.

'Maybe the frogs are still here,' Cosmo said, beginning to poke his nose amongst the debris on the floor. 'They might have hopped out of the incubator after it was tipped up. Let's look for them.'

They searched all over the room, but there were no frogs.

'This is terrible,' India mewed as the three cats left the laboratory and padded back up the basement stairs. Then, when they reached the kitchen again, they heard a familiar mewing at the back door.

'That's Father,' Cosmo said, rushing over to the closed door and mewing back. 'He doesn't sound very happy. Come on. We can get out to him through the window,' he miaowed to India and Kit, leaping up on to the nearest work surface and heading for the same open window he had used to enter the house on his previous visit.

As he jumped down and landed on the ground outside with a thud, he saw his father and Albert. The two cats were standing back to back miaowing indignantly –

and Cosmo let out a shocked hiss when he saw the reason why. Their tails had been tied together in a tight knot!

19

'Father! Albert! Who did this to you?' Cosmo miaowed, certain that the Frog-Witch would never treat a cat in such a manner (even if she did prefer frogs).

India jumped through the window at that point, and as soon as she saw Mephisto's poor knotted tail, she instantly forgot to be cross with him for deceiving her about the kittens. 'Mephisto! Don't try to move – you're just making it worse,' she miaowed, and she rushed over to lick the knot to see if she could slacken it a little.

'It's not an ordinary knot,' Mephisto warned her. 'It's a magic one.'

'Father, where's the Frog-Witch?' Cosmo asked anxiously. 'And where are all the frog-kittens?'

'The Frog-Witch has been kidnapped along with all your brothers and sisters,' Mephisto told him gruffly.

'*Kidnapped?*'

'Yes,' Albert joined in now, 'and I'm almost certain the kidnapper was the same young male witch we saw here this morning! He was wearing a mask, so I couldn't see his face, but he looked about the same height and build.'

'He was coming up the basement stairs when we got here, carrying a sack that was full of frogs, judging by all the croaking coming from it,' Mephisto continued. 'There was a green van parked outside the house, and the Frog-Witch was shouting for help from inside it. He must have shut her in there! We tried to pounce on him, but that's when he drew his wand from his pocket and did *this* to us! We couldn't do anything to stop him after that! He just got into his van and drove off!'

'We were just making for the garden shed, because I know that's where the Frog-Witch

81

keeps her broomstick,' Albert added.

'I thought that would be the quickest way to get home under the circumstances,' Mephisto said, 'though I don't know *how* we're going to untie our tails without Goody there to brew up a spell for us. We'll need more than a magic sneeze to untie *this* knot.'

'Why don't we go and see Bunty,' India suggested. 'Surely *she'll* know what to do, and we'll be able to tell her everything since she understands Cat.' (Goody's sister, Bunty, was a very clever witch who had often helped the cats in the past.)

'Good idea,' Mephisto agreed. 'Cosmo, go and see if the Frog-Witch's broom is in her shed and whether there's a basket we can attach for your mother and Kit.' (Non-witch-cats couldn't ride on broomsticks, but they could be transported on one if a basket was hooked over the end.)

'But we know who the kidnapper is!' Cosmo burst out. 'It's Amy's new boyfriend! So shouldn't we go straight to her house and see if he's there?'

'Not without Bunty,' India said sharply.

'Your mother's right,' Mephisto said firmly. 'Anyway, there's not much I can do with my tail like this. We must go to Bunty's house first. Now hurry up and fetch the broom, Cosmo. There's no time to lose!'

As the cats were flying towards Bunty's house on the Frog-Witch's broomstick, Selina Slaughter was talking on the prison telephone. The witches were each allowed to make one phone call a week, and Selina was holding the receiver close to her ear and speaking in a hushed voice as she asked, 'Well? What news?'

'She wouldn't give me the spell recipe,

and I couldn't find it anywhere in her house. Then she told me she had memorized it, not written it down. So I kidnapped her – *and* some of her frogs! She was fussing over them in her laboratory and they seemed like they might be especially important for some reason. Anyway, I've threatened to turn *her* into a frog, unless she tells me the secret recipe.'

'Excellent!' Selina was so excited that she failed to register a second witch entering the room and positioning herself at the next phone along.

'There's just one thing . . .'

'*What?*' Selina demanded, no longer whispering.

'Well, when I threatened her, she didn't react *exactly* as I'd expected.'

'What do you mean?'

'She said she's always thought it would be

rather *nice* to be a frog, and that she imagines pond life to be extremely relaxing.'

'She's bluffing!'

'I'm not so sure. She's totally batty about the horrid little creatures! Ever since I kidnapped her, she's been sitting with them on her lap, stroking them and telling them not to worry!'

Selina screwed up her forehead, thinking hard. 'How many of her frogs have you captured?'

'Eight.'

'Well . . .' Selina started to snigger. 'Perhaps a *better* form of persuasion would be to threaten to harm *them* rather than her. Why not tell her you'll squash them one by one in front of her – unless she hands over the spell. Tell her you'll stamp on one frog every hour until she agrees! If she's as potty about them as you say, that should do the trick!'

'Brilliant!' There was a short pause. 'But there's one other thing . . . I still haven't managed to find your friend Sybil and—'

'I told you already,' Selina interrupted impatiently, 'just find the nearest pond to where she used to live and she'll be there! Frogs who have once been witches don't know that they were ever anything other than frogs, but they are left with a special witch *instinct* that means they *always* return to familiar territory.'

'Yes, but even if I find the right pond, how do I recognize her? I mean, it will be *full* of frogs!'

'Don't you know *anything*?' Selina snapped. 'All frogs who have once been witches have a green, sparkly spot on their tummy, where their green belly button used to be. Now go and get on with it for goodness sake!'

It was only then that she noticed Murdina

Broom standing at the next phone along. Murdina's eyes were bright with excitement as she leaned across and whispered, 'I know you're up to something, Selina! And if you don't tell me what it is, I'll repeat *everything* I just heard to the prison warden!'

Panicking, Selina quickly ended her call. 'You mustn't say a word about this to anyone, Murdina,' she hissed back.

'Why shouldn't I?' Murdina snapped. 'You haven't exactly been friendly to me, you know!'

'Yes . . . well . . . if you keep quiet, I'll let you join me when I escape from prison.'

'*Escape?*' Murdina was astounded.

'Yes! We'll be turned into frogs first, like your sister and Sybil, but it won't matter. You see, I am about to obtain a brand-new spell that can change mutant frogs back into witches again!'

87

'*Never!*' Murdina's warty lips were starting to tremble with excitement.

Selina nodded. 'Just think, Murdina, in a few hours from now, you and I will be free witches again!'

'Free to be as bad as we like!' Murdina exclaimed.

'Exactly!' And the two witches began to cackle together quietly, so that anyone would think they were the best of friends.

6

'Mephisto! What's happened to you?' Scarlett exclaimed as she opened the front door at her aunt's house and saw the cats. But since Scarlett didn't speak Cat there was no point in the cats trying to answer her.

Bunty was in the kitchen, cooking up a wart spell in her cauldron. 'The witch next door has a terribly small wart on her nose and she wants me to make it bigger for her,' Bunty explained to her visitors. 'Personally I'm not a great fan of warts, but it's amazing the number of witches who are.'

'Look at Mephisto and Albert's tails, Aunt Bunty!' Scarlett prompted her.

Bunty, who until then had been focusing only on what was happening inside her cauldron, turned to look. 'Oh my goodness!'

she burst out in dismay. 'How did this happen?'

'It's a long story,' Mephisto replied, sitting down back to back with Albert on the kitchen rug. And he started by telling Bunty about the Frog-Witch's secret spell.

'But no witch has ever succeeded in making such a spell!' Bunty exclaimed. 'There have been lots of attempts over the years, but so far any claims to have actually *done* it have all turned out to be false alarms!'

'Well, I certainly hope *this* isn't a false alarm,' India miaowed sharply.

Mephisto quickly explained how the kittens had accidently been turned into frogs – and how when he and Albert had gone to the Frog-Witch's house to speak to her about it, they had witnessed the Frog-Witch being kidnapped.

'And when we tried to stop the kidnapper

he did *this* to us,' Mephisto finished, angrily swishing both his own tail and Albert's.

Bunty was looking very worried. 'This is terrible! If the Frog-Witch really *has* made a spell that can change frogs back into their previous forms, then it's very important that it isn't allowed to get into the wrong hands.' She frowned. 'I think I had better call an emergency meeting of the Good Witches' Society!'

'Yes – and don't forget to tell them that my kittens were kidnapped too,' India miaowed shrilly. 'They are *just* as important as the Frog-Witch.' She glared at Mephisto, who in her opinion had been neglecting to highlight that fact.

'Of course they are, India,' Bunty said at once. She swiftly explained everything to Scarlett, adding, 'Let us empty the cauldron of the wart spell, so that I can make an unknotting

91

spell for Mephisto and Albert's tails. Then I shall phone the GWS and see if anyone has any ideas who this kidnapper might be.'

'I already *know* who he is,' Cosmo told her impatiently. 'His name is Maurice and he's staying in the house next door to ours. He's pretending to be Amy's boyfriend!'

Bunty looked shocked. 'Are you quite sure?'

'Oh yes,' Cosmo began. 'You see—'

But unfortunately, at that moment, Mephisto's nose started to feel tickly. Everyone had forgotten that he had a cold, and now they all looked at him in alarm as his nose started to twitch.

'Don't sneeze near the cauldron, Mephisto,' Bunty warned him urgently, but it was already too late.

'A-A-A-*TCHOO*!' Mephisto let out the most enormous sneeze all over the kitchen.

As some of the magic droplets landed inside Bunty's cauldron, they reacted with the ingredients of the wart spell, and the cauldron liquid started to bubble more furiously. Suddenly there was a loud BANG! and stars with warts on them started to shoot out everywhere.

'Duck everybody!' Bunty shouted, as the warty stars whizzed about all over the room, causing warts to start growing on every surface they touched.

By the time the magic had fizzled out, there was a large wart on the door of the fridge, another three growing up from the surface of the kitchen table, several on the walls and a great big one on Albert's nose.

'Don't worry, Albert, we'll soon get rid of that for you,' Bunty attempted to reassure him.

But Albert was already growling furiously at Mephisto, whose whiskers were trembling with barely concealed mirth as he twisted round to look at the other witch-cat's face.

'Let's all go into the living room while Bunty is brewing up her unknotting spell,' India said hastily. 'You too, Kit. I don't think any of us should stay near that cauldron for one moment longer.'

'Except for Cosmo,' Bunty said. 'I shall need some witch-cat help with my spell, and Jet has gone to help my mother make an anti-wrinkle potion.' (Bunty's own witch-cat, Jet, had exceptionally potent sneezes, and she often lent him out to various friends and relatives.)

95

'I'm sure *my* magic sneezes are *almost* as powerful as Jet's now,' Cosmo mewed earnestly.

Bunty smiled at him and said that she was sure he was right, but that she would use two of his sneezes just to be on the safe side. 'They have to come from a witch-cat whose tail *isn't* in a knot,' she explained, 'which is why I can't use your father's or Albert's. Now tell me everything you know about this witch who you think might be the kidnapper, Cosmo.'

As the other cats left the kitchen, Cosmo started to tell Bunty about his two encounters with Maurice.

'Well, he certainly sounds like he could be involved,' Bunty agreed as she helped Scarlett pour the contents of the cauldron into some big jars before starting to pull down various unknotting-spell ingredients from her kitchen cupboards. 'We'd better use some serpent spit,' she told them. 'That's very good for dealing with anything snake-shaped, like a cat's tail. And we'll need several spoonfuls of sunlight to get the spell going nice and quickly – luckily I recently bought a new tin of that. And I shall need a pinch of fur from each knotted tail. Scarlett, when you've finished with the cauldron, could you go and comb Albert and Mephisto until you've got enough, please?'

'Yes, Aunt Bunty,' Scarlett said as she used a generous dose of magic cleaning spray on the cauldron. (That was a very important thing to do between spells if you didn't want traces of the previous spell contaminating the current one – which in this case could involve the cats ending up with warty tails as well as unknotted ones.)

Soon the unknotting spell was ready and Bunty called Mephisto and Albert back into the kitchen and helped them up on to the table, where she had already placed a steaming bowl of the spell liquid, covered with a towel.

'I want you to stand so that the joined part of your tails is over the bowl,' she said, removing the towel. 'Good. Now I will replace the towel over the knot in your tails.'

'What about my nose?' grumbled Albert.

'Don't worry,' Bunty said. 'We've got some wart-shrinking ointment up in the bathroom. It's very easy to shrink a wart.'

'I don't just want to *shrink* it,' Albert mewed indignantly. 'I want it removed altogether!'

'It will only be a very tiny speck afterwards,' Bunty promised him. 'You'll never know it's there. I had three on *my* nose before I shrunk them down, didn't I, Scarlett?'

All the cats looked in surprise at Scarlett's aunt who, with her rosy cheeks and golden hair, was really very pretty. There were certainly no signs of any warts – or even specks that might once have been warts – on her perfect skin.

'All right then,' Albert grunted. 'But it had better work.' And as he spoke, he suddenly felt his tail come free from Mephisto's.

The towel fell back over the bowl as both cats pulled their separated tails completely out from under it, miaowing with relief at being free again.

'Wonderful!' said Bunty. 'Now . . . if you will just sort out Albert's nose for him, Scarlett, I'll go and phone the head of the GWS. And after that I think I shall pay Maurice a visit.'

As Bunty was making her phone call, Amy

and Maurice were sitting in Amy's kitchen eating an early supper while Felina and Mia waited for them to finish so that they could lick their plates clean afterwards.

Felina had been very concerned on Amy's behalf ever since she had learned that Maurice was a witch, and she had become even more worried when Mia had followed Maurice outside into the garden just before supper-time – and returned with some news about him that was more alarming still. Now, as the young couple ate together (with Amy staring sickeningly into Maurice's eyes the whole time), Felina suddenly thought of a way to warn Amy that her new boyfriend was not what he seemed.

There was an almost-full bowl of cat crunchies in the kitchen, so Felina immediately set to work. Since she was an expert in written human language, it hardly took her any time to knock some of the crunchies on to the floor and tap them about until they formed human letters that spelled out the word W-I-T-C-H. Then, just to make things even clearer, she added an arrow

that pointed from the crunchy word to the chair where Maurice was sitting.

Her plan would have worked perfectly if Maurice hadn't been the first to get up from the table. As soon as he looked down and saw what Felina had written, his face went bright red. Then he trampled all over the crunchy letters, glaring furiously at the professor-cat.

'What's wrong, darling?' Amy asked in the especially doting voice she had previously reserved only for her cats.

'Your cats have just tipped their food bowl out all over the floor,' he snapped. 'Messy creatures! Never mind. I'll soon clear it up for you.' And he went to the cupboard to fetch the dustpan and brush. 'Let's go out for dessert,' he suggested. 'I'm sick of staying in the house with these wretched cats staring at us the whole time!'

'*Wretched* cats?' Amy's voice quavered

slightly, but she didn't say any more than that – which was unbelievable considering how fiercely Amy usually defended her beloved cats no matter what.

'I wonder if he can have hypnotized her in some way,' Felina whispered to Mia as they watched Maurice fetch Amy's coat and help her into it.

'Or put a spell on her,' Mia added.

Since neither Felina nor Mia was a witch-cat, they were unsure about the exact sorts of spells witches could put on humans, but they were certain that *something* had been done to Amy. Otherwise she would never have allowed Maurice to insult them like that. With Amy, her cats always came first. At least they always had done until now . . .

7

By the time Bunty arrived at Amy's house, Amy and Maurice had already left. After receiving no reply upon ringing the bell, Bunty went round to the back door, where Felina and Mia immediately appeared at the cat flap.

'They've both gone out,' Felina told her. 'I don't know where to.'

'Cosmo thinks Maurice might have kidnapped the Frog-Witch,' Bunty said, quickly filling the two cats in on what had happened. When she got to the part about the kittens being changed into frogs and also kidnapped, Felina and Mia both hissed loudly with shock. Bunty was forced to pause before gently adding, 'Have *you* seen or heard anything to suggest that Maurice might be involved?'

'He's certainly been coming and going a lot today,' Felina replied, swishing her tail from side to side as she attempted to control her mounting agitation. 'But he hasn't brought any witches or frogs back to our house. Mia, you'd better tell Bunty what you found out this afternoon.'

Shyly Mia related how she had followed Maurice after he had got back from his bus journey to the Witch Prison. He had gone out into the back garden and she had watched him climb over the bottom fence into the garden of Ramses the dog. There she had continued to watch as he searched the pond for frogs. 'Whenever he found one, he picked it up and turned it upside down to look at its belly,' she mewed. 'Then he put each one back in the pond. Finally he let out a big sigh and said, "Where *are* you, Aunt Sybil?"'

Mia paused to allow Bunty to digest this

amazing news, as Felina gave her daughter a half-protective, half-proud lick on the head.

'*Aunt* Sybil?' Bunty was looking stunned. 'I had no idea that Sybil had a nephew!'

'I don't think Cosmo knows either,' Mia said.

'But why is Maurice trying to *find* her? In frog-form she's no use to him whatsoever . . . unless . . .' Bunty frowned. 'Could he have heard about the Frog-Witch's secret spell and be intending to change Sybil back into a witch again? That would certainly give him a motive for the kidnapping. Of course, we still don't have any definite proof that he *is* the kidnapper.'

'Maurice certainly seems *very* interested in spells involving frogs,' Felina miaowed. 'Cosmo asked us to search Maurice's things and I found a lot of newspaper and magazine cuttings about frog magic – almost as though he was *researching* the subject.'

'Felina, I need you to let me know as soon as Maurice and Amy return to the house,' Bunty told the professor-cat. She frowned. 'But let's think . . . how are you going to contact me?'

'I shall use the telephone of course!' Felina mewed.

Bunty thought for a moment that Felina might be joking, but quickly remembered that the professor-cat could not only read human numbers, but had perfected the art of knocking the telephone on to the floor and holding a pen between her teeth to press the appropriate buttons.

'That's wonderful, Felina. I shall write down the number of the Good Witches' Society for you. I have arranged a meeting with them to see what I can find out about Sybil's nephew.'

'All right, but I'm sure Amy knows nothing about this kidnapping,' Felina replied. 'She's far too kind to be involved in anything like that.'

'*We* think Maurice must have put some sort of spell on *her*,' Mia added anxiously.

'Clearly, the sooner I confront Maurice about all this, the better,' Bunty said. She looked very grave as she continued, 'There's something else I want to make you aware of, Felina. You see, I think it is very unlikely that the Frog-Witch's spell will actually work – though obviously her kidnapper must *think* that it will.' She paused. 'India doesn't know that yet.'

Felina quickly saw what she was getting at. 'In that case, India and Mephisto's kittens won't be able to be brought back from frog-form either,' she said.

'Exactly,' Bunty responded sadly. 'And I

dread to think how India will react if that happens.'

Felina shuddered at the thought of the kittens having to stay as frogs forever, and she couldn't even begin to imagine how India would feel. And not for the first time the professor-cat found herself thinking that magic and kittens just wasn't a sensible combination.

As soon as Bunty told Cosmo and his family the news about Maurice being Sybil's nephew, they were horrified. They had known about Sybil's evil mother, Euphemia (who had met her end as a puff of smoke when one of her evil spells had gone wrong), but they had always thought that Sybil had no other relatives.

'It all makes sense now, why Maurice would kidnap the Frog-Witch,' Cosmo said.

And he felt the fur on his back stand on end as he thought about all the awful things Sybil might do, if Maurice used the secret spell to change his aunt back into a witch again.

'We still have to prove he truly *is* the kidnapper, Cosmo,' Bunty said. 'Though I have to say that it's sounding more and more likely. That's why I'm going to use the computer at the Good Witches' Society to see what I can find out about him. If he *has* kidnapped the Frog-Witch, then the more we find out about *him*, the better chance we have of finding *her*.'

'I am very worried about my kittens,' India mewed anxiously. 'It's getting dark now and they've never been out in the dark before.'

'Remember that they're frogs at the moment, India, and I'm sure frogs are quite used to the dark,' Bunty tried to reassure her.

'Even so, we can't just sit here and do

nothing!' India miaowed. 'Mephisto, you and I must go out tonight and speak to all the other cats in the neighbourhood. You never know – one of them might have seen this green van you spoke of.'

'That sounds like a very good idea,' Bunty agreed quickly, 'though I'd wear something over your nose and mouth, Mephisto, just in case you have another sneezing fit while you're out. Scarlett, why don't you make some posters showing this green van? I've got some glow-in-the-dark green paint at home, so all the witches and cats who are out and about tonight will be able to see it.'

'I'll help you with the posters, Scarlett,' Albert volunteered. 'I have a very good memory and I'm sure I can describe the van exactly.'

'What can *I* do to help?' Cosmo asked eagerly.

'You must stay here and look after Kit,' India told him swiftly. 'I don't want *him* going missing as well.'

'That's not fair!' Cosmo complained indignantly, but everyone ignored him as Bunty left the house on her broomstick, taking Scarlett and Albert with her.

*

'It's really stupid that I have to stay home with you, Kit,' Cosmo grumbled in a frustrated mew after Mephisto and India had also left. (Mephisto had first wrapped himself in a brand-new silk scarf of Goody's that would hopefully catch any stray sneeze droplets should the need arise.)

'You don't *have* to stay, Cosmo,' Kit miaowed back confidently. 'You can leave me here on my own if you want and I promise I won't tell Mother and Father.'

It was a tempting offer, but when Cosmo thought of all the trouble Kit might get into if he was left in the house without any supervision, he decided it probably wasn't worth the risk. 'I do know *something* we can both do instead of just waiting in the house,' he said.

'Does it involve magic?' Kit asked excitedly.

'No – but it involves some special detective work! You see, I've been thinking . . .' Cosmo paused importantly for a few moments. 'Remember that big nasty frog who scared you and made you fall into the pond this morning?'

Kit nodded, shivering slightly at the memory.

'Well, what if *that* was Sybil? I mean, that pond is the nearest one to her old house, so it makes sense that she'd return there.'

'But if you're right, wouldn't Maurice have found her when *he* went to the pond?' Kit pointed out.

'Maybe he just didn't look hard enough. After all, it's much easier for *us* to search for her, because we can get right underneath all the bushes.'

'Let's go and look for her now then!' Kit exclaimed, bounding enthusiastically over to the cat flap, only to stop short the second he had pushed it open with his nose. 'It's ever so dark outside, Cosmo,' he said nervously. 'How will we see anything?'

'Cats can see very well in the dark, silly!' Cosmo told him. 'In fact, the night-time is the *best* time for cats to go out! But I'm hungry! Let's have some supper first. Then we'll go.'

'Cosmo, what will we *do* with Sybil if we find her?' Kit asked as he joined his older brother at the bowl of dried food Scarlett had filled for them before she left.

'I'll pick her up in my mouth and carry her back to the house,' Cosmo mumbled, between bites of cat crunchies. 'Then we can take turns guarding her until Bunty gets back.'

115

'That sounds fun!' Kit miaowed. 'We'll be guard *cats* instead of guard dogs! Ooh – I really hope we find her! We're looking for a very *big* frog with a bright green belly button, right?'

'We're looking for a very big *ugly* frog with a bright green belly button,' Cosmo corrected him. Because one thing he was still absolutely sure of was that Sybil couldn't possibly look any more attractive in frog-form than she had done as a witch.

Just as they were about to set off for the pond, Mia arrived.

'Has Maurice come back already?' Cosmo asked, feeling his tail start to go bushy.

'No, not yet,' Mia mewed. 'I just came over to see how you two were getting on.'

'We're about to go down to the pond to look for Sybil ourselves,' Cosmo confided.

'We think Maurice might have missed her when he looked there earlier.'

'I'll come too then!' Mia said.

So they all left the house together and set off down the garden, with Kit dashing ahead at top speed, mewing loudly about how exciting it must be to hunt things during the night like grown-up cats.

'Wait for us when you get to the bottom fence,' Cosmo called out to him, but by the time Cosmo and Mia reached the fence themselves, Kit had disappeared.

The next thing they heard was a loud yapping.

'Shush, Ramses! It's only us!' Mia yapped back at him. Mia's mother had already taught Mia to speak Dog, since (as the professor-cat was fond of saying) it was rather an unsophisticated language and therefore very simple to learn.

117

'Is that you, Mia?' Ramses demanded suspiciously.

'Yes – and your other neighbour, Cosmo. And the little kitten is Cosmo's brother. Is he in your garden, by the way?'

'Why else do you think I'm barking like this?' Ramses replied impatiently. 'He's no right to come into my garden without my permission.' He let out a little growl, because he found all cats highly irritating, even if they *were* Yorkie-sized and understood how nice it was to sit on a human's lap – something that most other dogs just couldn't seem to grasp. 'What are you doing here?' he demanded as Cosmo and Mia jumped over the fence to join Kit, who was cowering behind a tree trunk, keeping well away from the excitable Yorkie.

'We wanted to have a look in your pond,' Mia said.

'*Everyone* wants to look in my pond today,' Ramses told her. 'I've had two strange humans nosing around in it already! I was shut inside the house away from my dog flap at the time, so all I could do was bark at them from the window.'

'*Two* strange humans?' Mia queried in surprise.

'That's right. First there was a young man with a scowly face who came and turned over all the frogs to look at their

119

bellies. He actually stole one of them too! Slipped it into his pocket – bold as you like!'

'Wait a minute . . . are you absolutely sure that he took one with him?' Mia asked anxiously.

'Yes! I yapped at him that they were *my* frogs, not his, but he just ignored me! Then there was a second young man who came soon after the first – and *he* did the very same thing! Only he didn't help himself to any frogs as far as I could tell – he just looked at them all.'

'And you're sure they were two *different* men?'

'Of course I'm sure! They both had dark hair and they were the same sort of size, but the first one came from the street and the second one came in just like you did, through the back garden.'

'Could they have been witches rather than humans, do you think?'

'I suppose so,' Ramses replied. 'Humans and witches all look the same to me!'

Mia quickly translated all this from dog-yap into cat-miaow so that Cosmo and Kit could understand it.

'But that doesn't make any sense!' Cosmo exclaimed. 'The man who came in from the back garden must have been Maurice, but who can the *other* man be? And if he actually *took* a frog from the pond, then does that mean that *he* found Sybil?'

Just then they heard an urgent miaowing coming from their own side of the fence. 'Mia! Cosmo! Where are you?'

'That's Mother,' Mia said.

'Maybe Maurice is back!' Cosmo mewed. 'Come on. We'd better go and see!' He miaowed his thanks to Ramses, which Mia

121

quickly translated, and then the three cats jumped back over the fence into Cosmo's garden.

Felina was standing in the middle of the lawn, and as soon as she saw them she called out loudly, 'Maurice and Amy have just returned home. I've already phoned Bunty and she's on her way back.'

'Oooh – *please* can *I* come over to your house and help guard him until Bunty gets here?' Kit begged, sounding like he was ready to explode with excitement.

'This isn't a game, Kit,' Felina replied sternly. 'Maurice is a very dangerous witch and we must all stay well away from him!' And she ordered all three kittens back inside Cosmo's house, to wait there with her until Bunty returned.

8

Bunty was carrying her strongest wand when she arrived back at Cosmo's house, along with Scarlett and Albert.

'I have looked up Sybil's family on the Witch Computer,' she told the cats. 'Apparently Sybil has a half-sister, who has a son called Maurice. I shall go and call on him right now and find out what he has to say for himself.'

Cosmo wondered whether he ought to tell her about the second young man Ramses had seen at the pond, but decided to wait and let her interview Maurice first. He was so sure that Maurice was the kidnapper that he didn't want to say anything that might put her off the scent.

'I'll stay here and send these out,' Scarlett

offered as she and Albert showed the others the pile of glow-in-the-dark posters they had made. Each one had a fluorescent picture of a green van on the front, together with the words: HAVE YOU SEEN THIS VEHICLE?

'Thank you, Scarlett,' Bunty said. 'And after that, I really think you should try and get some sleep. It's way past your bedtime.'

'Sleep sounds like an excellent idea to me,' Albert agreed, yawning loudly. 'I think I'll just have a quick bite to eat first – got to keep my strength up you know – and then go for a little nap upstairs.'

'Be careful, Aunt Bunty,' Scarlett said as her aunt made to leave with Felina.

'Don't worry, Scarlett, I shall have my wand fully charged the whole time,' Bunty replied as she exited through the front door. 'And it's not as though Maurice will be expecting me at this time of night, so I shall definitely have the advantage.'

As soon as Bunty and Felina had gone, Cosmo, Mia and Kit jumped up on to the kitchen table to watch Scarlett set up the spell which would make the posters fly off and stick themselves to various neighbourhood lamp posts and other suitable surfaces.

'We *could* make the posters actually *speak* to any witches who pass by,' Scarlett told them, 'but Aunt Bunty thinks it might alarm any humans who happen to be passing too.'

125

As Albert munched away greedily at the remains of the Crunchy-munchies, the three younger cats watched with bated breath as Scarlett unscrewed the lid from a bottle containing a ready-made leaflet-distribution spell. 'Mother was going to use this to send out some leaflets advertising the kittens when they're old enough to go to new homes,' she said as she used a glass pipette to suck up several drops of the gold-coloured liquid. 'All I need to do is put one drop on each poster.'

Kit felt his stomach lurch as she spoke and he had to struggle not to let out a distressed little mew. It wasn't that it was news to him that Goody eventually intended to find new homes for him and his siblings – that was always what happened when mother cats gave birth to large litters. But unlike his brothers and sisters who were all quite excited by the idea, Kit couldn't bear the thought of leaving.

Cosmo didn't notice that Kit was upset, because he was completely preoccupied with a worry of his own. He couldn't stop thinking about what Ramses had told them earlier. Perhaps he ought to have mentioned it to Bunty before she confronted Maurice, he thought, and since Albert was the only grown-up cat present he decided to tell him instead.

'Mia and I went to the garden pond tonight,' he miaowed. 'We saw Ramses there, and he said he saw another man as well as Maurice looking in his pond for frogs today.'

'Yes,' Mia joined in now, 'and he saw *that* young man actually *steal* a frog from the pond.'

'Well, why on earth didn't you say so before?' Albert said, so taken aback that he actually paused between mouthfuls of cat munchies. 'Clearly someone *else* is also trying to find Sybil. But who?'

'I don't know. That's the trouble,' Cosmo said. 'But what if it's someone who *also* knows about the Frog-Witch's spell and who *also* wants to turn Sybil back into a witch again?'

Albert looked puzzled as he pointed out, 'Yes, but if so how are all these other witches finding out about the spell? I'm sure the Frog-Witch can only have told one or two very close friends she really trusts about it, if anyone.'

'Or *cats* she really trusts!' Cosmo said. 'After all, she told *you*, didn't she, Albert?' He stared at the older cat, suddenly struck by the thought that Albert was quite a gossipy sort of cat. 'Albert, *you* didn't tell anyone else about the spell, did you?' he miaowed anxiously.

'Of course not!' Albert growled. 'What do you take me for?'

'Oh, I'm sure you didn't tell any *witches*,' Cosmo continued swiftly, 'but did you happen to mention it to any other *cats*?'

Albert scowled at him. 'Certainly not! Apart from my oldest and most loyal friend, George-of-the-park, that is, who I would trust with my life . . . in fact with all *nine* of my lives . . . It's rumoured that we have the same father, you know . . . though my mother always said she couldn't be certain . . . George does have a white moustache like mine but then—'

'*When* did you tell him, Albert?' Cosmo interrupted sharply.

'Oh, I don't know . . . it must have been a few weeks ago . . . I think it was just after I discovered that Selina Slaughter's house was empty . . . I invited George to stay there

129

with me for the night so we could have a bit of a catch-up. He'd just found a very nice chicken carcass in one of the park bins that he offered to share with me . . . *that's* how good a friend he is . . .' Albert licked his lips at the memory.

'Well, I think you'd better go and ask him straight away if *he* told anyone else,' Cosmo said.

'What? Right *now*?'

'Yes,' said Cosmo. 'It's important, Albert! The kittens are depending on us! And so is the Frog-Witch!'

'All right, all right . . .' Albert grumbled. 'Though George is not the least bit sociable and he hardly ever speaks to other cats, so I'm sure there's nothing to worry about.'

As Albert left through the cat flap, Scarlett was opening the kitchen window to allow the posters (which had all sprouted

golden wings)
to fly off into
the night.
'Let's hope
somebody
recognizes the
van, and contacts
us,' she said as she
watched them flutter
off in different directions.

Cosmo hoped so too, but he couldn't help thinking that rather a lot of the local residents probably owned green vans, since green was a favourite colour among witches.

It was half an hour or so later, after Scarlett had gone to bed and the cats were still waiting for both Albert and Bunty to return, that Kit discovered an old mousehole in the kitchen. As he sniffed at it curiously he asked his brother, 'Cosmo, could a *frog* fit inside one of these, do you think?'

'I suppose so. Why?' Cosmo asked.

'Well, I was thinking that maybe my brothers and sisters could find a mousehole like this one and hide in it,' Kit said. 'Then their kidnapper wouldn't be able to hurt them.'

Cosmo was about to respond when he was suddenly struck by something. He stared at the mousehole, murmuring, 'Of course . . .'

'Of course, *what?*' Mia asked, padding over to join him.

'Albert said he was in Selina Slaughter's cottage when he told George-of-the-park about the Frog-Witch's spell, didn't he?' Cosmo miaowed.

'Yes,' Mia and Kit both replied, wondering what was coming next.

'Well, what if Selina's *white mice* overheard him? They could easily still be spying for Selina and reporting back to her whenever they visit her in prison! What if *they* told Selina about the Frog-Witch's spell and *she's* the one who arranged for the Frog-Witch to be kidnapped?'

Mia looked at Cosmo in horror, knowing only too well what evil deeds Selina Slaughter was capable of.

'Who *is* Selina Slaughter?' Kit asked curiously.

'She's a very bad witch who was a close friend of Sybil's,' Cosmo told him. 'She tried to help Sybil escape from prison just before you were born – they were planning on setting up a Bad Witches' Society and they were going to do all sorts of horrible spells together.'

133

'Maurice could have been visiting *Selina* when he caught the bus to the Witch Prison this afternoon!' Mia pointed out. 'The two of them could be working together. It all fits.'

'Come on!' said Cosmo. 'Let's go and tell Bunty!'

9

Before they even had time to reach the cat flap they heard the sound of a key in the front door and suddenly Amy entered the house, accompanied by Felina.

'Amy has come to babysit for Scarlett,' Felina said. 'Bunty has gone off to visit some other witch with Maurice – and she told me to let you know that Maurice *isn't* the kidnapper!'

'But he must be!' Mia exclaimed. 'He went to the Witch Prison today to visit Selina Slaughter which means he must be working for her. You see Selina has some white mice she uses as spies and—'

'Maurice *didn't* visit Selina,' Felina interrupted her sharply. 'Listen and I'll explain everything . . .'

*

For the last hour, Bunty had been interviewing Maurice very carefully in Amy's living room. It was after midnight and Amy had already gone to bed by the time Bunty got there, which meant that they didn't have to worry about being overheard, except by Felina, who was lying on the back of the sofa pretending to be asleep.

'So what if I *am* Sybil's nephew?' Maurice had burst out indignantly as soon as Bunty had challenged him with that fact. 'I'm not proud of it – and I'm only looking for her so that I can capture her and make sure she *doesn't* get turned back into a witch again! And I don't know anything about the Frog-Witch being kidnapped – though it doesn't surprise me to tell you the truth!'

'I already know that you went to see the Frog-Witch today,' Bunty continued, keeping her hand on the wand inside her pocket just in case Maurice decided to make any sudden moves. 'What do you know about her secret spell?'

Maurice sat down heavily on the nearest chair at that point, and let out an exasperated sigh. 'I went to see her to warn her that if her spell fell into the wrong hands it could prove dangerous. I wanted her to destroy it, but of course she refused! Like I just said, I'm not surprised she's been kidnapped. She was asking for trouble inventing a spell like that!'

'How did you come to hear about her spell in the first place?' Bunty asked suspiciously.

'The Frog-Witch and my mother have a mutual friend. *She* knew about the spell and told my mother about it.'

'Your mother being Sybil's sister?'

'*Half*-sister, yes. My mother's father took her away from her mother – an extremely evil witch called Euphemia – when she was just a baby. Euphemia later met Sybil's father and had Sybil. My mother never had any contact with her mother *or* Sybil after that. She was always frightened that Euphemia might try to find her and she was very relieved when she heard about Euphemia being turned into a puff of smoke and Sybil being sent to prison. She was even more pleased when she heard that Sybil had been turned into a frog while trying to escape. But my poor mother has always been a very nervous sort of a person, and when she heard recently about the Frog-Witch's new spell, she became obsessed with the idea that someone might use it to turn Sybil back into witch-form again. She went to see the Frog-Witch herself and begged her to destroy the spell, but the Frog-Witch wouldn't hear of it. So I thought it would put my mother's mind at rest if I could somehow capture Sybil while she's still a frog, and make sure that she stays that way!'

Bunty looked thoughtful. 'And since witch-frogs are known to return to familiar territory, you knew that your best chance of finding her was to search close to where she used to live.'

'That's right. Getting Amy to fall in love with me seemed like the easiest way of checking out the area without anyone knowing who I really was. I was afraid that if anyone discovered I was Sybil's nephew, they would assume I was up to no good – just like you did.'

Bunty glanced at Felina, who was still curled up in the same position. 'I suppose you used some kind of love potion on Amy?' she said disapprovingly.

'Yes. I had to use a much more powerful one than I'd intended, because her love for her cats was so strong that it was interfering with my spell.'

'Yes . . . well . . . Amy has always been extremely devoted to her cats,' Bunty murmured.

'*Ridiculously* devoted, if you ask me,' Maurice grunted, at which point

Felina's eyes snapped open.

'Actually we *didn't* ask you,' she mewed, letting out a rude hiss, which was completely lost on Maurice since he didn't understand Cat.

'There's just one more thing,' Bunty continued quickly. 'Mia told me you caught the bus to the Witch Prison this afternoon . . .'

'That's right. I went to see the Prison Warden,' Maurice said. 'I wanted to make sure she knew about the Frog-Witch's spell because of how it might affect the prison tagging device that turns witches into frogs if they try to escape. I told her I don't think the tags will be much of a deterrent any more, once all the prisoners find out that there's a new spell that can turn frogs back into witches again.'

'What did the warden say to that?' Bunty asked curiously.

'She said she didn't believe such a spell could work and that she wasn't going to change Prison policy on account of a far-fetched rumour.'

'Oh dear,' Bunty murmured, looking worried. She stayed silent for a few moments, frowning as if she was trying to think what to do next. Finally she let out a loud sigh and said, 'The trouble is that I now have no idea whatsoever who the Frog-Witch's kidnapper might be.'

'You mean I was your only suspect?'

'I'm afraid so.'

Maurice looked thoughtful. 'Well the kidnapper *must* be someone who also knew about her secret spell. Who else might she have told, do you think?'

'I really don't know. That's the problem.'

'Perhaps we should go and speak to my mother's friend,' Maurice suggested. 'She's been friends with the Frog-Witch for a long time, so she might be able to tell us who else the Frog-Witch is likely to have confided in besides her. I can take you to her house right now if you like.'

'It's very late,' Bunty said. 'Can't we just phone her?'

'Unfortunately not. She's rather eccentric – my mother reckons that's why she and the Frog-Witch get on so well – and she doesn't believe in using human inventions like telephones.'

'I see. Well, does she live very far away?'

'A fair distance, but if we set off now by broomstick, we should get there by morning.'

'Then we'd better leave at once. I wonder . . .' Bunty looked uncomfortable as she asked, 'Do you think Amy could be persuaded to babysit for Scarlett while

143

I'm gone? I know she's already gone to bed herself, but I really don't like to leave Scarlett in the house on her own all night and—'

'Amy will gladly do anything I ask her to,' Maurice interrupted, 'as long as I hold off giving her the antidote to that love potion, of course.'

'Well . . .' Bunty looked a little sheepish as she mumbled, 'Perhaps it wouldn't hurt to hold off giving her the antidote until tomorrow . . .'

'Fine,' Maurice said. 'I'll go and wake her up right now.'

And Bunty avoided making eye contact with Felina, who had now jumped down from the sofa and was sitting very pointedly between Bunty and the door, glaring at her furiously.

*

After Felina had explained everything to Cosmo and Mia, Cosmo couldn't believe it at first. He had been so sure that Maurice was the kidnapper that it was hard to accept straight away that he had been wrong.

Mia, however, was much quicker to adjust her thinking. 'Selina could easily have somebody *else* working for her,' she blurted out immediately. 'Like that other male witch Ramses saw at the pond today – the one who put a frog in his pocket. I wonder who *he* was. I really wish we'd told Bunty about him, don't you?'

Cosmo's tail was starting to bush up as he remembered something. 'Selina Slaughter has a son,' he told them. 'He was moving into Sticky-End Cottage when Albert took me there earlier. What if *he's* the witch who came to the pond and took the frog?'

'If only we had a photograph of him,

145

we could show it to Ramses and ask him,' Mia said.

'I've got a better idea!' Cosmo exclaimed, his whiskers jerking forward keenly. 'Why don't I fly Ramses to Sticky-End Cottage on Goody's broomstick so that he can actually *see* Selina's son for himself? That way we'll know for sure.'

'That sounds highly dangerous to me,' Felina miaowed, sounding very disapproving.

'Yes, and we don't know if Ramses will agree to it,' Mia pointed out. 'I mean, have you ever seen a *dog* riding a broomstick before?'

'A Yorkie isn't that much bigger than a cat,' Cosmo said. 'He'll easily fit into the basket at the front. Don't worry. I'll take really good care of him so he'll be quite safe.'

'*I* think it's a brilliant idea, Cosmo!' exclaimed Kit, swishing his tail from side to side excitedly.

'Yes – but *you're* not coming,' Cosmo told him immediately. 'And neither is Mia. There won't be enough room in the basket for all of you.' 'Quite right,' Felina said firmly. 'You must stay here with me, Mia. Broomsticks are a quite unsuitable form of transport for any ordinary cat – as I have told you many times before.'

147

'But I'll *have* to go with Cosmo,' Mia protested. 'How else will he and Ramses be able to understand each other?'

'All Ramses has to do is let me know if Selina's son is the same witch he saw at the pond or not,' Cosmo said. 'He can give one bark for yes and two for no. It'll be easy.'

'I'm not so sure, Cosmo,' Mia began, but she was interrupted by Amy (who of course was completely oblivious to the cats' conversation) announcing that she was going upstairs to sleep in the spare room and that any cat who wanted to come with her would be very welcome.

'I shall be up in a little while,' Felina mewed back.

'You go upstairs too, Kit,' Cosmo told his little brother quickly.

'But *I* want to go with you, Cosmo,' Kit whined.

'You must do as you're told, Kit,' the professor-cat told him sternly, tapping him sharply on his hind leg to send him upstairs after Amy. 'As for you, Mia, you may go with Cosmo to explain everything to Ramses, but after that you must come straight back here. In fact, I shall come out and wait for you in the garden, so don't take too long about it!'

10

It was pitch black outside as the moon was now completely hidden by clouds, but Cosmo and Mia's eyes soon adjusted to the dark as they bounded down the back garden and over the bottom fence. Ramses would probably have gone to bed by now – he always slept in his basket in the kitchen – but since he had a dog flap, which was left open for him at night, the cats were fairly sure they'd have no problem reaching him.

'I hope he doesn't start yapping as soon as he hears us, and wake everybody up,' Cosmo said, because it was a well-known fact that dogs never stopped to think before they barked.

As soon as they reached the back door, Mia gently pushed open the dog flap and mewed very softly, 'Ramses? Are you there? It's Mia and Cosmo!'

They heard a surprised whimper, then a short yap, at which point Mia slipped the rest of her body through the flap and called out to Ramses, 'Shush! We don't want to wake up your humans!'

Ramses immediately left his basket and trotted across to the back door. 'Please don't come any further,' he warned her. 'I don't want the whole place smelling of cats!'

After Mia had translated this, Cosmo (who had now entered the kitchen himself) was about to point out indignantly that he and Mia were not in the least bit smelly, but he decided not to waste any time arguing. 'Just tell him why we're here, Mia,' he said. 'And see if he'll help us.'

Cosmo waited while Mia explained everything to Ramses. Fortunately, at the mention of going for a ride on a broomstick, Ramses got very excited.

'I've always wanted to go for a ride up in the sky!' he told Mia. 'Perhaps we could visit the moon if there's time! And I'm sure my humans would be very impressed if I fetched them one of those stars as a souvenir!'

'The moon and the stars are a very long way away, Ramses,' Mia told him patiently, 'much further than they seem when you look at them from the earth. But I'm sure you'll be able to find *something* interesting to bring back with you.'

Ramses readily followed the two cats out of the house and down the garden, only just managing to refrain from yapping loudly with excitement as they bounded over the grass together. Then, when they reached the bottom fence, they all stopped abruptly as they realized that Ramses couldn't jump over it.

'Wait here with Mia while I go and fetch the broom,' Cosmo told him – and while Mia was repeating this in her best Dog yap, Cosmo jumped over the fence and trotted back towards his own house.

Felina met him at the top of the garden, and when he told her what had happened, she insisted on going to join her daughter and Ramses while Cosmo went to fetch Goody's broomstick.

Goody always kept her broomstick in the hall, whereas the basket was kept in the porch so that the cats could have access to it whenever they needed. First Cosmo started up the broomstick by using a magic sneeze on the bristles. Then he commanded it out through the cat flap and round to the front porch to join the basket. By the time Cosmo reached the porch, the broom and the basket were already attached, and Cosmo was pleased to see that the lovely warm blanket that India always insisted on wrapping around herself whenever she flew anywhere was also inside the basket. That should please Ramses, he thought, and keep him from getting too cold when they got up above the rooftops.

Cosmo quickly climbed aboard the broomstick and directed it to the bottom of Ramses's garden. And he was very glad that it was now so dark that no one was likely to see them and ask why a witch-cat and a Yorkshire terrier were taking a broomstick ride together in the middle of the night.

Despite the fact that Mia and Felina had both given Ramses strict instructions to only bark when he saw Selina's son, the little dog started yapping almost as soon as they left the ground. At first Cosmo thought it was because he was so excited, but after they had been in the air for several minutes it was clear that Ramses was barking for another reason.

Under the blanket that Ramses was sitting on, something was moving. Ramses was getting more and more agitated, clawing at the blanket and yapping more and more loudly until finally a small black nose pushed

155

its way out from under the cover and a familiar voice mewed, 'It's all right! It's only me!'

'Kit!' Cosmo exclaimed crossly. 'What are you doing here? I told you to stay at home with the others!'

'I know, Cosmo – but I really wanted to come with you!' Kit extracted himself from the blanket as Ramses yapped something in his ear that he didn't understand, but which sounded very rude.

Luckily the moon came out from behind a cloud at that moment, and Ramses stopped yapping and looked up at it in awe. Then, completely transfixed by the view all around him, he stood up on his hind legs with his front paws resting on the front of the basket, and let out a low, thrilled sort of growl as the wind blew back the shaggy hair from his face. He was clearly having the time of

his life, and as they passed over rooftop after rooftop he looked down on each one and gave a little yelp of pleasure.

Cosmo miaowed a greeting as another broom flew by with a family of witch-cats on board, all of whom stared in amazement at Ramses. The smallest kitten looked like it might have fallen off the broom in shock if it hadn't been held so firmly by its mother.

157

'Being a witch-cat must be the most exciting thing in the world!' Kit exclaimed. 'Oh – I really hope I pass the magic witch-cat test like you did, Cosmo! Then I can ride on the broom instead of just inside the basket. Maybe if I try I can even balance on the broom now ...' And before anyone could stop him he was scrambling over Ramses's head and reaching up out of the basket to try and grab at the broomstick handle with his paws.

Ramses barked crossly and Kit fell backwards into the basket again, at which point Ramses sat on him. And no matter how much Kit wriggled to get free after that, he found that he was firmly pinned down by the Yorkie's bottom for the rest of the journey.

'Here's Sticky-End Cottage,' Cosmo mewed when they finally arrived at the house which Selina's son and daughter-in-law had moved into earlier that day. 'And look! There's a green van parked in the driveway!'

He lowered the broom towards the garden, planning to make a noise outside that would hopefully make Selina's son show himself, but Cosmo had forgotten about the other new resident of the cottage. There was no need for Cosmo to make any noise at all, because an angry-looking guard

159

dog appeared in the garden (thankfully chained to its kennel) and began to bark furiously at them. Ramses immediately started to bark back, and when Selina's son stuck his head out of the bedroom window to see what was going on, Ramses kept yapping – not once or twice as he was meant to, but over and over again so that it was impossible to tell if he recognized Selina's son or not.

Then, just as Cosmo was guiding the broom safely upwards away from the house, Selina's son produced a wand from his dressing-gown pocket and pointed it at the broomstick, mumbling a whole string of magic words at the same time. A bright beam of green light shot out from the wand like a laser, and connected itself to the bristle end of the broom, which also started to glow green. Then the broom stopped moving

forward and started to be drawn backwards towards the house.

'I need to do a magic sneeze on the bristles to break the spell,' Cosmo mewed, starting to panic. 'Quick! I need some dust to breathe in!' But there was no dust on the broomstick or in the basket, and however hard Cosmo tried to make himself sneeze without it, he couldn't.

The broom landed with a bump in the back garden and Selina's son came running out of the house with a big net, which he threw over them.

'Who is it?' his wife called out from the back door.

'Witch-cats! And some horrid little dog by the look of things. Well, I know just what to do with *him*!' Selina's son lifted the net and grabbed Ramses (who was still yapping hysterically) by his collar, hauling him out. 'Sid will look after you, won't you, boy?' And he attached the terrified Yorkie to the same chain as the guard dog.

'Let him go! He hasn't done anything wrong – and neither have we!' Cosmo miaowed, hoping that Selina's son might understand Cat.

'I don't know what you're saying, so you may as well shut up,' the angry young witch replied, picking up the whole net and carrying the struggling bundle into the house with him. 'I'm going to put these two with the others,' he told his wife.

'Do you have to bring them inside, Spencer?' she complained. 'You know I can't stand cats.'

'Yes I do,' Spencer replied firmly. 'They might be spies and they might not – but as my mother would say, it doesn't do to take any chances.'

'I'm sick of hearing about what your mother would say,' Spencer's wife snapped at him. 'You always do exactly what she tells you and I don't see why. You're a grown man – not a child! Why are you so scared of her?'

163

'I'm *not* scared of her,' Spencer retorted sulkily. 'I just think it's safer not to upset her too much, that's all. I mean, it's going to be bad enough if she ever finds out the truth about *you*!' And with that, he brushed past his wife and headed for the living room, keeping a tight grip on the net containing the two cats.

Cosmo had been inside Sticky-End Cottage before – when Selina had lived there – and on that occasion he had discovered her basement, which could only be accessed via a secret reverse chimney that led downwards from the fireplace in the living room. So it was no surprise to him when Selina's son opened up the magic chimney entrance and Cosmo found himself being thrown down the chimney chute into the basement along with Kit.

They landed on a large cushion and narrowly escaped being squashed by Spencer, who came hurtling down the chimney passage just behind them. 'You can go in the cage with my other visitors until I decide what to do with you,' he said nastily.

Cosmo looked up and saw a large cage on one side of the room. He recognized the cage from the last time he had been in the basement – and he knew that a magic sneeze wouldn't be powerful enough to unlock it. There was a stool inside the cage, and sitting on the stool, looking very sorry for herself, was the Frog-Witch.

'Cosmo!' she cried out as soon as she saw him.

'Oh, so you two *do* know each other,' Spencer said slyly. 'I suspected as much! Thought you'd try and rescue her, did you, puss?' And he started to laugh as he unlocked

the cage with a
special magic
key and
hurled
the two
cats, who
were still
tangled
up in the
netting,
inside.

Then he stepped into
a pair of special shoes that had rocket
thrusters attached to the heels, and went
zooming back up the reverse chimney into
the main house, the magic key placed firmly
in his pocket.

'Cosmo, what are you doing here?' the
Frog-Witch exclaimed as she untangled
the two cats from the mesh net.

'We were trying to find out if Selina's son was the witch who kidnapped you,' Cosmo replied. 'And obviously he *is*!'

'Where are my brothers and sisters?' Kit asked in a frightened voice.

'Oh, they're all hopping around the basement somewhere,' the Frog-Witch told him. 'This cage can't contain frogs, so I've told them to hide as best they can. It's difficult though, because the rest of the room is so empty.'

Kit immediately saw that she was right. There was no furniture in the basement apart from the cage they were in – if you could call that furniture. And now that his eyes were more accustomed to the darkness it was easy to spot the little frogs cowering at the edges of the room, or hopping around in vain looking for cover. It seemed that there were no mouseholes anywhere.

167

'Look at
that big frog!'
Kit suddenly
mewed,
pointing across
the room at a
transparent plastic
container that had
air holes in the
lid. Inside it, a very
large frog with a wart on its face and very
angry eyes was sitting on its own, croaking
loudly. As they watched, it suddenly gave a
massive hop upwards, hurling itself against
the container lid as if it was trying to
escape.

'Apparently that's Sybil,' the Frog-Witch
told them. 'Spencer wants to use my new
spell to turn her back into a witch again.'

Cosmo miaowed that on no account

must the Frog-Witch do that.

'I know, my dear, but I'm afraid it's not that simple,' the Frog-Witch replied. And she began to explain that Spencer had threatened to squash one frog every hour from first light in the morning, unless she handed over her spell.

'Oh no!' mewed Kit, gazing helplessly through the bars at the frogs, who it was hard to believe had been seven kittens and one white mouse just a few hours earlier.

'Apparently, after the spell has been tested on Sybil, Selina is going to try and escape from prison too. She'll be turned into a frog in the process, of course, but Spencer will turn her back into herself again straight away using my spell.'

'That's terrible!' Cosmo miaowed. 'We can't let it happen!'

'I know,' the Frog-Witch replied. 'But

169

what choice do I have? If I don't do as he asks, he'll squash all your brothers and sisters – not that he realizes they *are* your brothers and sisters of course – and he won't release me. And I *must* be released so that I can go home and attend to my pet frogs. I'm particularly worried about my frog prince – he's locked in his cage, so he won't be able to get out and forage for food like the others. Goodness knows what his father will say if he dies of starvation while he's in my care.'

'His father?' Cosmo queried in surprise.

'His father is a witch-king called King Three-Toes who rules over a land a long way away from here. After his son was turned into a frog by a wicked spell, he brought him to me and asked me to look after him until the day when I would be able to turn him back into a prince again. He has promised me a very large reward if I succeed in doing that – money which I intend to use to fund further frog research.'

Cosmo listened to all this with interest, and as he listened he found that he was starting to get an idea. He sat silently for quite some time until his idea was fully thought out and then, just as first light was starting to dawn outside (though the occupants of the basement had no way of knowing that), he told his idea to Kit and the Frog-Witch.

'You're so clever, Cosmo!' Kit gushed, looking admiringly at his big brother.

'It might not work, of course,' Cosmo mewed cautiously.

'I think it's a very good idea, Cosmo,' the Frog-Witch told him, frowning as she added, 'if only I can convince Spencer to go along with it.'

171

11

At daybreak, Spencer listened with a suspicious expression on his face as the Frog-Witch outlined her new proposition.

'If you let me and my friends go, I will give you something much better than my spell recipe,' she told him. And she explained all about the reward money King Three-Toes had promised her in exchange for the safe return of his son. 'If you do as I ask, then after I have changed the frog prince back into his normal self, I will hand him over to you and *you* can take him back to his father and collect the reward.'

Spencer frowned, clearly not fully convinced that she wasn't trying to trick him. 'Witch-princes are known to be extremely powerful,' he said. 'I would never be able to keep him a prisoner once you changed him back.'

'Oh yes you would,' Cosmo put in quickly. 'He's a *baby* prince you see. So long as you have a basket to carry him in you can easily take him back to the king on your broomstick.'

Since Spencer couldn't understand Cat, the Frog-Witch had to translate this for him.

'How do I know you're not lying?' Spencer asked.

'When we get to my house I'll show you the press cuttings sent to me by the witch-king when he entrusted his son into my care,' the Frog-Witch said. 'The news articles all clearly state that the prince was a four-month-old baby when the tragedy occurred.'

'Hmm . . . well . . . we do already have a Moses basket ready for our own baby to

173

sleep in when it arrives,' Spencer murmured, looking thoughtful. 'And we certainly have plenty of baby blankets we could wrap him in.'

'See – it's as if it was meant to be!' the Frog-Witch exclaimed, beaming at him encouragingly.

'Yes, but what about my mother – and her friend Sybil?' Spencer glanced over at the large frog that was glaring at him from inside its plastic container. He was fairly certain that the frog couldn't understand him, but even so, its eyes made him feel quite unsettled.

'Just tell your mother the spell didn't work,' the Frog-Witch replied. 'Then she'll have to stay in prison and you can have this house all to yourself – or you can even buy a bigger one with all the money you'll be getting from the witch-king. If you ask me you'll be much happier *without* your mother bossing you about all the time.'

Spencer frowned thoughtfully, for it was true that his mother could be very interfering. It was something he and his wife often argued about. 'I think I'd better go and discuss this with my wife,' he said.

'Very well, but don't take too long about it,' the Frog-Witch told him. 'And remember that my offer only stands if these two cats and all my frogs are released along with me!'

'And Ramses too,' Cosmo reminded her, desperately hoping that the little dog was still all right.

Twenty minutes later Cosmo, Kit and the Frog-Witch (who had four frogs in each pocket) were all standing outside in the back garden, being guarded by Spencer, who was pointing his wand at them. Its green tip

175

was glowing just enough to let them know that it was fully charged as he waited for his wife to emerge from the house with the Moses basket and baby blankets.

'We'll have to be careful,' the Frog-Witch whispered to the cats. 'That wand Spencer keeps pointing at us belongs to Selina, and it's a very powerful one.'

'Hurry up and get on with it,' Spencer barked at the Frog-Witch, who was about to upturn Sybil's container on to the grass.

'Do we *have* to let Sybil go?' Cosmo had asked disappointedly when she had told Spencer that *that* was one of her conditions too. 'I mean, if you won't let Spencer squash *her*, couldn't we at least keep her as our prisoner instead?'

But the Frog-Witch had been adamant that no frog (even one that had previously been a bad witch) was to be killed, or deprived of its freedom without good reason, if she could possibly help it.

'After all, she is quite harmless now, even if what remains of her old bad-witch instinct does make her more ill-tempered than other frogs,' the Frog-Witch said as they watched Sybil hop away towards the nearest rhubarb patch, looking like she would readily trample any smaller frogs that got in her way. 'Come on,' she added as Sybil finally disappeared from view. 'Let's collect your little Yorkie friend and get going.'

Spencer went over to the dog kennel and called out Sid's name, but there was no reply. He stooped down to look inside and saw Sid and Ramses curled up together fast asleep, the Yorkie resting his head on the guard dog's tummy.

'Some guard dog you are!' Spencer complained, and he was about to prod the

sleeping Sid between the ribs with his wand when Ramses woke up and began to yap ferociously at him.

'It looks like the two of them have become friends,' the Frog-Witch said. 'I think it might be best if we just unclip them from that chain and leave them here for now. We can always come back and collect Ramses later.'

'Yes, but they're going to need some

breakfast while we're gone,' Cosmo pointed out, because for the first time he couldn't help noticing that Sid looked extremely underfed.

So the Frog-Witch asked Spencer to put down a large bowl of food for the dogs – promising that this would definitely be the last of her demands – before they all set off for the Frog-Witch's house together. Spencer and his wife were travelling on their own broom, which had been fitted with an extremely wide chair to allow Spencer's pregnant wife to ride in comfort.

The first thing the Frog-Witch did on reaching her own house was to rush into the living room and check on the frog prince. He was still inside his cage, croaking loudly, and the Frog-Witch said she must feed him immediately.

'We can't have you being transformed

179

back into a prince on an empty stomach, can we, my precious?' she crooned at him.

'How do I know you're speaking the truth about his father being willing to pay lots of money for him?' Spencer asked, watching in disgust as the Frog-Witch picked up a jar of slugs from the sideboard and unscrewed the lid.

'You don't have to take *my* word for it – I'll give you his phone number and you can give him a call,' the Frog-Witch replied, going over to her desk to find her address book. At the same time she handed Spencer a small envelope of *Witch News* press cuttings, which had pictures of the baby prince taken just prior to his being turned into a frog twenty years before.

While Spencer made his telephone call to the king, the Frog-Witch announced that she must take the frog prince down to her laboratory immediately. She still had the eight other frogs in the pockets of her coat, having slipped them some slugs to eat too, and as she headed for the basement stairs she told Spencer's wife that it would probably be safest if she remained where she was. 'It's not that I'm *expecting* anything to go wrong with my transformation spell, my dear, but I really don't think you should take any risks in your condition. After all, we wouldn't want you giving birth to a frog instead of a baby, would we?'

Spencer's wife looked horrified and immediately said she would wait in the hall.

'Very sensible – and please ask Spencer to do the same,' the Frog-Witch said. 'It might spoil my concentration if he's looking over my shoulder, and then the spell won't work. The cats can assist me if I need any help, and you needn't worry about any of us escaping because there's no other way out of my basement, as your husband has already discovered when he kidnapped me.'

Before Spencer's wife had time to reply, the Frog-Witch had disappeared down the basement stairs, with Cosmo and Kit following at her heels. But as they reached the door of her laboratory, she frowned and whispered to the cats, 'You know, I really don't trust those two. I think it might be best if one of you went back to keep an eye on them – without letting them know you're there of course.'

'Spy on them you mean?' Kit mewed excitedly. '*I* can do that!'

'Be careful, Kit. Make sure they don't

see you,' Cosmo warned as Kit turned to scamper back up the stairs again.

'It's probably just as well that *he's* safely out of the way too,' the Frog-Witch murmured as she stepped inside her laboratory. She let out a loud sigh as she saw the mess it was in. 'Come on, Cosmo, let's get this cleared up,' she said. 'And after that we can start brewing up my spell!'

While Cosmo was helping the Frog-Witch in her laboratory, Kit had crept back up the basement stairs to the hall and positioned himself under the large chair that Spencer's wife was sitting in as she waited for her husband to finish his phone call.

'The Frog-Witch was speaking the truth!' Spencer exclaimed, sounding delighted as he rejoined his wife. 'We're going to be rich at last!' Apparently the witch-king had

183

been more than happy to offer Spencer the same huge amount of money that he had previously offered the Frog-Witch in exchange for the safe return of his son (who Spencer had promised to deliver to the king that same day).

'And I'll tell you something else.' Spencer lowered his voice so that Kit had to prick up his ears to hear him clearly. 'As soon as the Frog-Witch has performed her spell and handed over the baby prince, we'll capture her again and make her give us the spell recipe as well. If she refuses, we'll squash all those frogs right in front of her, just to show her we mean business. Then we'll keep on squashing all the frogs in this house and garden until she gives in.' He sniggered. 'I don't see why we shouldn't get the money *and* the spell, do you?!'

As Kit listened to this, his first thought was to report back to Cosmo and the Frog-Witch without delay. He crept out from the cover of his chair and padded as lightly as possible across the hall, failing to notice two frogs hopping across it in the opposite direction on their way upstairs. He let out a startled miaow as he collided with them, and his miaow – together with the indignant croaking of the frogs – caught Spencer and his wife's attention immediately. Before Kit had time to escape, Spencer had bent down and scooped up the terrified kitten.

'Thought you'd spy on us again, did you?' Spencer said, as he dangled Kit by the scruff of his neck.

'Please don't hurt me,' Kit mewed in a panic. But of course neither Spencer nor his wife could understand him, and even if they had they wouldn't have taken any notice.

185

'Let's shut him somewhere until this is all over,' Spencer suggested. 'There's a shed in the garden. We can put him in there.'

'I'll take him,' his wife replied. 'You'd better get down to the basement and listen outside the door to see if you can hear what they're up to.'

After her husband had gone, Spencer's wife carried Kit, who was still mewing loudly and struggling to get free, outside to the garden shed, where her gaze fell upon an

empty sack. She looked at Kit thoughtfully for a moment. Why leave this detestable kitten in the shed to be rescued later by his friends, when there was a far more gratifying alternative?

'In you go,' she told Kit as she shoved him inside the sack and tied a knot in it.

She took the sack to the biggest pond in the garden – which she assumed was also the deepest – and swung it to and fro a couple of times before tossing it into the water, where it landed with a loud splash.

'I should have put something heavy inside to make sure it sinks,' she thought, frowning at her own absent-mindedness.

To her relief, however, the more Kit struggled inside the sack, the more it soaked up the water and the heavier it became in the process. And as she walked away from the pond, she was confident that it wouldn't be long before Kit drowned in a perfectly satisfactory manner, despite her silly oversight.

12

While his wife was dealing with Kit, Spencer was creeping down the basement stairs towards the Frog-Witch's laboratory. His wand was fully charged and ready to do whatever he commanded it, but he wanted to give the Frog-Witch time to complete her spell before he burst in on her.

After he had waited patiently for what felt like forever, he finally heard the sound he had been hoping for – the crying of a baby. The frog prince had clearly been turned back into his true form and it was time for Spencer to claim him.

'You'd better let me in now!' he shouted through the door, and at the same time he tried the handle. But the door wouldn't budge, which must mean the Frog-Witch

189

had locked it. 'It's no use trying to keep me out – I can easily use my wand to open this door,' he warned her.

'Just a few more minutes, Spencer,' the Frog-Witch called back to him. 'We have to keep the baby warm until he's fully adjusted to the transformation – if I open the door it will create a draught.'

The baby had stopped crying now and Spencer could hear a lot of movement inside the locked room – as if the Frog-Witch was rushing about.

'There, there, little prince,' he could hear her crooning. 'I know it's a bit of a shock to your system, but you'll soon get used to your new shape.'

'If he's cold, why don't you wrap him in that baby blanket we gave you?' Spencer snapped impatiently. 'Now hurry up and open this door! I want to see him!'

It was less than a minute later when he heard the bolt being pulled back on the other side of the door. Then the door was flung open and the Frog-Witch stood there looking triumphant.

'It worked!' she declared, beaming from ear to ear. 'My transformation spell actually worked!'

Spencer pushed past her to look inside the room. 'Where is he then?' he demanded.

'Here I am!' said a cross-sounding male voice. And Spencer turned to see, not a baby, but a fully grown prince, whose hair, eyebrows and curly moustache were all green, and who had the baby blanket wrapped like a towel around his waist.

Spencer's mouth fell open, but no words came out, as the Frog-Witch told him, 'The prince *was* a baby when he was turned into a frog – but that was twenty years ago. We've

191

just watched him change from a frog, to a baby, then to a little boy, then to a twenty-year-old young man, haven't we, Cosmo? It was quite a transformation, I can tell you! Even the king doesn't know that he's now got a grown-up son! I must say I suspected that would be the case, but until I had tried out my spell I couldn't be sure!'

As the Frog-Witch was speaking, the prince had stepped forward and snatched Spencer's wand, and in his royal hand the green tip glowed even brighter and then began to fizz like a sparkler on Bonfire Night.

'I shall phone the Good Witches' Society and ask them to come and arrest Spencer straight away, if you'll be good enough to guard him for me, Your Highness,' the Frog-Witch said.

'It will be my pleasure,' the prince said, keeping the wand pointed at Spencer as he

193

ordered him up the stairs ahead of the Frog-Witch.

Cosmo, who had been watching everything from a safe corner of the room, miaowed, 'Wait for me!' before bounding after them.

Spencer's wife gasped in shock when she saw the prince, and as the Frog-Witch made her telephone call Cosmo called for Kit to come out of hiding.

Strangely there was no reply, so after searching for him in the rest of the house, Cosmo returned to the living room and asked if anyone had seen him.

The Frog-Witch had finished her phone call by this time, and since she was the only one present who could understand Cat, she translated Cosmo's question, at which point Spencer's wife let out a nasty laugh.

'You're too late to save *that* little pest I'm afraid!' she sneered.

'Why? What have you done to him?' the Frog-Witch demanded.

'Unfortunately, not a lot,' Spencer grunted sourly. 'He's locked up in the garden shed, that's all.' (It was a well-known fact that no witch could ever actually *kill* a cat, due to an ancient Witch Law that meant they would be turned into a puff of smoke if they did – which was what had happened to Sybil's mother, Euphemia.)

But Spencer's wife had a very strange look on her face. 'That's what *you* think,' she said impatiently. 'Your silly witch rules don't apply to me – and that means I can do whatever I like!'

'What are you talking about?' the Frog-Witch asked, clearly confused.

Spencer blushed self-consciously as he mumbled, 'Actually my wife isn't a witch, she's a human. We've had to pretend she's a

195

witch, because we didn't want my mother to find out. Mother doesn't approve of mixed marriages, you see . . .'

'I *do* see.' The Frog-Witch looked horrified as she turned slowly to face Spencer's wife again. 'So what exactly *have* you done with Kit?'

'I've drowned him of course! He's inside a sack at the bottom of that nice deep pond in your garden!'

Cosmo immediately hissed with shock, and all the colour drained from the Frog-Witch's face as she said hoarsely, 'Come with me, Cosmo.' And they rushed out into the garden to the sound of Spencer's wife's mocking laughter.

When they got outside they saw at once that the shed door had been left open. 'Well, he's certainly not in here,' the Frog-Witch said, sticking her head inside very briefly.

'Look!' Cosmo cried out, pointing to the biggest garden pond.

Right in the centre of it a brown sack seemed to be floating on top of the water.

'It looks like it's resting on a gigantic green leaf,' Cosmo mewed.

'I don't think it's a *leaf*,' the Frog-Witch murmured.

And sure enough, as they got closer, they saw that the sack was being held afloat by a green raft made up entirely of frogs.

'Who says frogs aren't clever creatures?' the Frog-Witch exclaimed in wonderment as the frog-raft started to glide across the water towards them.

'Kit – are you in there?' Cosmo called out, but the sack remained silent and motionless.

As soon as the bundle was within her reach, the Frog-Witch grabbed it and swung it out of the pond. Then she untied the sack and tipped it up gently on to the grass.

'Kit! Kit! Are you all right?' Cosmo mewed, rushing forward as the soggy kitten tumbled out on to the ground.

After one terrifying moment of silence, Kit let out a very faint mew.

'Oh, you poor little thing!' the Frog-Witch gasped, taking off her cardigan and wrapping Kit in it. 'We must take you inside and get you warmed up straight away.'

'Th-they w-wanted to . . . to . . .' Kit spluttered, but the Frog-Witch told him to save his breath.

'Don't worry, whatever they wanted to do, they didn't succeed,' she reassured him. 'We are all quite all right! And thanks to my clever frogs – so are you!'

After the Frog-Witch had carried Kit into the kitchen and rubbed him dry with a towel, Cosmo filled him in on everything that had happened. 'And, believe it or not, Spencer's wife *isn't* a witch, she's a human,' he finished, 'even though she eats mice – which *I've* never heard of *any* human doing before!'

'Of course I'm not nearly as much of an expert on humans as I am on frogs,' the Frog-Witch began thoughtfully, 'but I *have* heard that some of them get very strange

199

food cravings when they're pregnant.' She frowned as she added, 'You know, I really feel quite sorry for that baby, having those two for its parents, and Selina Slaughter for a grandmother.'

Cosmo's whiskers sprang forward anxiously at the mention of families. 'We still haven't changed my brothers and sisters back into kittens,' he said urgently. 'Can we do it *now*, do you think?'

'I don't see why not,' the Frog-Witch replied.

'Please can *I* help this time?' begged Kit, who was starting to feel much better already.

'I think it would be best if Cosmo is the *only* cat who knows the ingredients of my secret spell,' the Frog-Witch said. 'But if you want to see it in action, Kit, you are welcome to keep watch outside that air vent you found the other day – the one that leads into my laboratory. You mustn't get *too* close to it, mind, or you might find yourself getting more action than you bargained for!'

So, while the Frog-Witch went to check on the prince and his two prisoners, Cosmo took Kit outside. 'You must go no closer to the opening than this, Kit, do you understand?' Cosmo said as he showed his little brother where it would be safe for him to sit.

'Don't worry – I promise I won't move from this spot!' Kit replied excitedly.

Cosmo, who didn't trust his brother when he was looking that excited, quickly sniffed at some nearby loose grass to make the inside of his nose tickly.

'A-A-A-TCHOO!' he sneezed, sending magic droplets all over the ground between Kit and the air vent. 'If you *do* go any closer, all your fur will turn pink and you'll look very silly,' he told Kit sternly – and he only hoped that would be enough of a threat to make Kit do as he was told.

Cosmo's threat did help Kit keep his word to start off with, but by the time twenty uneventful minutes had passed, Kit was getting very fidgety. 'I bet Cosmo's having a much more exciting time than me in the Frog-Witch's laboratory,' he thought to himself, starting to feel quite cross. 'I mean, what am I waiting here *for* exactly?'

But just as he was thinking that, he heard a loud gushing sound coming from inside the vent – and at the same time he thought he heard the distant sound of croaking. Completely forgetting about Cosmo's magic sneeze, he was just lifting up one paw ready to move in closer when, all of a sudden, a huge cloud of sparkling green smoke came

bursting out of the air-vent opening and hurtled towards him! Totally caught by surprise, he only just managed to duck out of the way before the sparkly smoke cloud exploded into thousands of bright green stars that shot out in all directions – all of them croaking loudly! Then, as he continued to watch in disbelief, *kitten*-shaped puffs of green smoke started to billow out from the vent.

And down in the basement laboratory, the eight frogs were all letting out final indignant croaks as they were magically transformed by the Frog-Witch's new spell into one bright green mouse and seven bright green kittens!

13

That evening Selina Slaughter and Murdina Broom were sitting watching the *Witch News*, along with the other inmates of the local Witch Prison.

'It has just been confirmed that this morning a groundbreaking transformation spell was successfully performed for the first time!' the television newsreader announced. 'Unbelievable though it may seem, the spell has changed a frog back into a prince – and that prince is here with us in the studio now, along with his father, King Three-Toes.' The camera moved across to focus on the young prince (whose hair and moustache were still green) sitting beside his jubilant-looking father, who was wearing a gold crown with precious gems set in the sides of it, which he

205

only ever wore on very important occasions. 'Your Majesty, first let me ask *you* how it feels to be reunited with your son after twenty years ...' the newsreader prompted.

There then followed interviews with the king and the prince, both of whom enthusiastically praised the ingenuity of the Frog-Witch and described how she had looked after the prince in frog-form for many years, while working all the time on developing her new spell.

Then the Frog-Witch herself appeared, beaming with pride. She was accompanied by the Head of the Good Witches' Society who explained how the Frog-Witch had undergone the terrible ordeal of being kidnapped by Spencer Slaughter, who had thankfully now been arrested along with his wife.

'STUPID BOY!' Selina hissed as all eyes in the prison TV room turned to look at her.

'Shush!' one of the other witches snapped, because the Frog-Witch was now telling *her* side of the kidnap story.

'Of course, what Spencer *didn't* know,' the Frog-Witch explained, 'is that my spell has an inbuilt safety mechanism that means it will only work if *I* am the one performing it. So even if the spell recipe *is* stolen, no other witch but me will ever be able to make use of it.'

'Which brings me to my next question …' the news reporter continued, turning to the Head of the Good Witches' Society again. 'If this is the case, then might we not see further attempts to kidnap the Frog-Witch by those who want to force her to use the spell against her will?'

'Indeed we might,' the Head Witch replied gravely, 'which is why our Society has decided to take some very serious precautionary measures. Firstly we will we be monitoring the Frog-Witch's use of this spell very closely – and she has agreed not to perform it without first obtaining special permission from us. And secondly, in order to protect her from any further kidnap attempts, my colleagues and I have performed a special spell on *her*, which means that if anyone should attempt to harm, kidnap or threaten her in any way, that person will be instantly turned into a toad.' There was a pause while the TV viewers were allowed to digest this astonishing information.

'And as far as I am aware, no one has even *begun* to invent a spell that can change *toads* back into their previous forms!' the Frog-Witch added smugly.

As a lively discussion broke out among the prison witches, a shot of Spencer in handcuffs flashed up on the screen.

'Look, Selina – it's your son!' burst out Murdina Broom (who had been sitting very quietly until now, slowly taking in the unwelcome fact that she would no longer be escaping from prison).

'Spencer Slaughter will almost certainly

be joining his mother, Selina, in Witch Prison very shortly,' the reporter continued, 'but after today's shock admission by his wife, that she is in fact not a witch as previously claimed, but a *human*, it has been decided that she will be handed over to the appropriate human authorities. We understand that the Human Society for the Prevention of Cruelty to Animals is especially keen to interview her regarding the attempted drowning of a kitten, the malnourishment of her own dog and allegations of extreme cruelty to mice . . .'

The rest of the reporter's words were drowned out by the sound of all the prison inmates cackling with laughter.

'Selina has a *human* for a daughter-in-law!'

'Selina's grandchild will be half *human*! How revolting!'

'Just think – the baby might be born with a *human* belly button instead of a green one! Yuck!'

Selina herself was so overcome by this shocking news that she stayed frozen to her seat for several minutes, not even noticing that Murdina had crinkled up her nose

as if suddenly detecting a very bad smell,
before pointedly moving to a seat well away
from her.

But gradually the taunts of the other
witches did begin to register, and Selina
felt her face blush bright red as it became
all too clear to her that she was soon going
to be the laughing stock of the whole
prison.

The news reporter was talking now
about the brave rescue mission carried out
by Cosmo and his companions, at which
point Selina's eyes nearly bulged out of her
head and she stood up and shook her fist at
the television set.

'THAT WRETCHED COSMO!' she
shouted. 'I MIGHT HAVE KNOWN HE'D
BE BEHIND THIS!' And she was so furious
that she could hardly speak for spitting.

*

The following afternoon, India and Mephisto decided to celebrate the safe return of their kittens by holding a Kitten-Naming Ceremony in their back garden – with the Frog-Witch as Guest of Honour. The seven newly returned kittens still had green fur, but as the Frog-Witch had been quick to point out immediately after their transformation, the skin underneath their fur was a perfectly normal colour.

'It is merely a case of waiting for the green fur to fall out and normal fur to grow in its place,' she had reassured India, who had nevertheless done so much licking in an attempt to remove the green colour, that her tongue had become quite dry.

'It's the same for the prince – and for that little mouse I changed back to normal,' the Frog-Witch had added. 'But if you really can't wait for their fur to fall out,

213

you can always get it shaved off straight away at the vet's.'

India greatly distrusted the vet and couldn't bear the thought of him touching any of her kittens. 'I've decided that having green kittens for a little while is a small price to pay for getting them all back safe and sound,' she told the Frog-Witch now as she escorted her to the garden bench where Bunty was already sitting (having just arrived back from visiting Maurice and his mother, who had both been hugely relieved to hear that Sybil was to remain a frog after all).

'Though unfortunately it *does* mean they can hide from me in the grass much more easily,' India added as she hurried off to attend to her offspring, who were getting very fidgety as they sat on a row of upturned flowerpots waiting for the ceremony to begin.

Scarlett, who had just finished handing round glasses of lemonade and saucers of milk to all the guests, was sitting on the grass in front of the bench with Kit on her lap, stroking him under his chin. Kit wasn't taking part in the ceremony as it had been unanimously agreed that he should keep the name Kit since it suited him very well.

Kit was not only delighted to escape all the extra grooming, but had been especially happy ever since he had asked Bunty if she could speak to Goody about *not* finding a new home for him when the time came. 'My brothers and sisters are all quite pleased to be going to new homes,' he had told her. 'But *I* want to stay here! Surely *one* more cat in the family wouldn't be too many, would it?'

Bunty had given him an affectionate stroke on his head and said, 'I'm sure that Goody will let you stay here if that's what you really want, Kit. But you are also very welcome to come and live with Jet and me. And if you do turn out to be a witch-cat you can help us with our spells. Would you like that?'

'Oh, I'd like that *very* much!' Kit had replied, and ever since then he hadn't been able to stop purring.

Felina was sitting near by on the grass, purring too. Both she and Mia were feeling much happier now that Amy was back to normal. (Amy had asked Maurice to leave as soon as he had given her the love potion antidote, and now she had gone back to stroking and fussing her two cats in the same way that she had always done.)

As well as Felina and Mia, Cosmo's parents had invited Bunty's witch-cat, Jet, Albert-of-the-street (who had brought along his friend George-of-the-park) and several other neighbourhood cats to attend the Naming Ceremony. Cosmo had even sent Mia to ask if Ramses would like to come, but the little Yorkie had turned down the invitation, politely explaining that he was very much afraid he might find the smell of so many cats in one place rather overpowering. And in any case, he was extremely busy trying to persuade his humans to adopt his new friend, Sid, who was temporarily staying with him after being rescued from Sticky-End Cottage. (So far Ramses was howling horribly every time anyone tried to part him from the bigger dog, and his humans were now talking of going out to buy a bigger basket, which Ramses took as a promising sign.)

'Ladies and gentlemen, queen cats and tomcats, if I could have your attention, please . . .' Mephisto's loud miaow suddenly boomed out, and everyone immediately fell silent.

Mephisto's own attention was suddenly caught by a straggly bit of fur on his chest, which he stopped to lick into place, before announcing grandly, 'It is time to begin the Naming Ceremony!'

Then his nose started to twitch rather alarmingly and some of the cats in the front row started to look worried.

'A-A-A . . . !' he began, and everyone scattered in different directions to avoid his magic-sneeze droplets. But luckily no sneeze followed, and Mephisto, who had been relieved to wake up that morning feeling almost completely cold free, waited patiently for his audience to reassemble.

'We have invited the Frog-Witch here today,' he declared when everyone had got themselves settled into neat rows again, 'so that she can do us the honour of choosing names for the seven kittens you see in front of you.' He paused dramatically before adding, 'For as I am sure you are aware . . . these are no ordinary kittens!'

'You can say that again,' one of the neighbourhood moggy cats murmured to the cat sitting next to her. '*Green* kittens! I ask you . . . whatever will these witch-cats think up next?'

'These are the first kittens ever to have been turned into frogs *and back again*!' Mephisto finished triumphantly. And if his face hadn't been covered with black fur, he would have visibly flushed with pride.

As all the guests cheered or miaowed loudly, the Frog-Witch stood up and took a step forward. She made a short speech about the delightfulness of both frogs *and* kittens, before turning to Kit's seven brothers and sisters and beaming at them.

'It is a great honour for me to be invited to choose your names,' she told them, 'and I have given the matter my most careful consideration. As you may be aware, I particularly like names that begin with the letter "F".'

Cosmo, who was sitting beside Mia, whispered, 'Uh-oh,' in her ear, and she had to put her paw to her mouth to conceal a smirk.

As the seven kittens stepped forward, the Frog-Witch touched each one in turn on the head and solemnly announced, 'I hereby name you *Freddie . . . Freda . . . Frankie . . . Flora . . . Finlay . . . Freya . . .* and *Fiona!*'

The name choices were met with purrs and claps from all the cats and witches present, and a self-conscious twitching of whiskers from the kittens themselves. Then just as the Frog-Witch was about to say a few final words, the ceremony was interrupted by the sound of barking coming from the other side of the fence at the bottom of the garden.

'It's Ramses and Sid! What are they saying?' Cosmo asked Mia.

'They're saying they just saw a big ugly frog in their pond,' Mia replied, listening intently to the string of yaps. 'It had a wart on its face and very angry eyes, and they were just trying to flip it over to see if it had a green belly button when it hopped away from them!'

'Maybe it's Sybil!' Cosmo miaowed, feeling a nervous thrill run down his spine at the prospect of coming face to face once more with his least-favourite frog (who thankfully now had no chance of being turned back into his least-favourite witch).

Kit, who had overheard them, immediately jumped off Scarlett's lap, his tail bushing up in anticipation of another adventure. 'Come on, Cosmo!' he mewed. 'Let's go and see if we can catch her!' And without waiting for a reply he tore off down the garden.

'Come back, Kit!' India called after him in alarm. 'I don't want you going anywhere near that pond!'

'Don't worry, Mother. I'll make sure he's all right!' Cosmo miaowed back, and he let out an excited growl before racing off at top speed after his little brother.

**'A-A-A-TISHOO!' Cosmo burst out, sending a huge
shower of magic sneeze into the cauldron.**

Cosmo has always wanted to be a witch-cat, just like his
father, so when he passes the special test he's really excited.
He can't wait to use his magic sneeze to help Sybil the
witch mix her spells.

Sybil is very scary, with her green belly button and toenails,
and no one trusts her. So when she starts brewing a secret
spell recipe – and advertising for kittens – Cosmo and his
friend Scarlett begin to worry. Could Sybil be cooking up a
truly terrifying spell? And could the extra-special ingredient
be KITTENS?

A purr-fectly funny and spooky story starring one brave
kitten who finds himself in a cauldron-full of trouble.

Cosmo and the Great Witch Escape

'If this spell works,' Sybil cackled, 'the only ones getting turned into frogs will be pesky Cosmo and his family!'

Cosmo the witch-cat is delighted that evil Sybil – the most terrible of witches – is safely in prison. In fact, she's even been fitted with a special tag, which means that if she tries to escape she will be turned into a frog.

But then mysterious goings-on are reported on *Witch News*. Baby witches are being visited by strange midwives and having their long, curly toenails clipped and stolen. Cosmo is sure something sinister is afoot. Could a highly wily witch be brewing a spectacularly spooky spell?

Cosmo returns in this wonderful tale of magic and mystery.

Cosmo's Book of Spooky Fun

A bewitching book of quizzes and jokes!

Grab your broomstick and join the fun in this purr-fectly puzzle-packed book, featuring Cosmo the witch-cat and all your favourite characters from Gwyneth's spooky stories.

Fans of Cosmo will love this fun-packed book of bewitching puzzles and games.

Mermaid Magic

There's a secret world at the bottom of the sea!

Rani came to Tingle Reef when she was a baby mermaid – she was found fast asleep in a seashell, and nobody knows where she came from.

Now strange things keep happening to her – almost as if by magic. What's going on? Rani's pet sea horse, Roscoe, Octavius the octopus and a scary sea-witch help her find out . . .

fairy secrets

Ellie is delighted when she goes to visit her aunt and meets Myfanwy and Bronwen, the valley fairies.

And when the fairies invite Ellie to a meeting at the tiny toy museum in the village, she learns one of the biggest fairy secrets of all. With a little bit of fairy dust, toys can come to life!

But the museum is about to close, and with it the enchanted entrance to Fairyland. Can Ellie come up with a plan to save them all before it's too late?

Another brilliant adventure starring all your favourite fairy friends.

A selected list of titles available from Macmillan Children's Books

The prices shown below are correct at the time of going to press. However, Macmillan Publishers reserves the right to show new retail prices on covers, which may differ from those previously advertised.

Gwyneth Rees

Cosmo and the Magic Sneeze	978-0-330-43729-5	£4.99
Cosmo and the Great Witch Escape	978-0-330-43733-2	£4.99
Fairy Dust	978-0-330-41554-5	£4.99
Fairy Treasure	978-0-330-43730-1	£4.99
Fairy Dreams	978-0-330-43476-8	£4.99
Fairy Gold	978-0-330-43938-1	£4.99
Fairy Rescue	978-0-330-43971-8	£4.99
Fairy Secrets	978-0-330-44215-2	£4.99
Mermaid Magic (3 books in 1)	978-0-330-42632-9	£4.99
Cosmo's Book of Spooky Fun	978-0-330-45123-9	£4.99
The Magical Book of Fairy Fun	978-0-330-44421-7	£4.99

For older readers

The Mum Hunt	978-0-330-41012-0	£4.99
The Mum Detective	978-0-330-43453-9	£4.99
The Mum Mystery	978-0-330-44212-1	£4.99
My Mum's from Planet Pluto	978-0-330-43728-8	£4.99
The Making of May	978-0-330-43732-5	£4.99

All Pan Macmillan titles can be ordered from our website, www.panmacmillan.com, or from your local bookshop and are also available by post from:

Bookpost, PO Box 29, Douglas, Isle of Man IM99 1BQ

Credit cards accepted. For details:
Telephone: 01624 677237
Fax: 01624 670923
Email: bookshop@enterprise.net
www.bookpost.co.uk

Free postage and packing in the United Kingdom